THE VINEYARDS OF CALANETTI

Saying 'I do' under the Tuscan sun...

Deep in the Tuscan countryside nestles the picturesque village of Monte Calanetti. Famed for its world-renowned vineyards, the village is also home to the crumbling but beautiful Palazzo di Comparino. It's been empty for months, but rumours of a new owner are spreading like wildfire...and that's *before* the village is chosen as the setting for the royal wedding of the year!

It's going to be a roller coaster of a year, but will wedding bells ring out in Monte Calanetti for anyone else?

Find out in this fabulously heart-warming, uplifting and thrillingly romantic new eight-book continuity from Mills & Boon® Romance!

Dear Reader,

I have loved every book I've written (well, nearly every book…). But sometimes a book just sets itself apart. That's what happened with Dani and Rafe's story.

Dani won my heart with her can-do attitude, in spite of the tragic beginnings to her life. But Rafe was a little different. He's a grouchy perfectionist. True, he's a very good-looking grouch, but he's still a grouch. That is until Dani begins to uncover his soft side…or maybe until he can't resist *showing* Dani his soft side.

I'm a firm believer that love is more mental than physical. We're drawn to people who bring out the best in us. Dani might be the one getting promotions, but Rafe's really the one whose whole world changes when Dani walks through the doors of Mancini's!

I hope you love this story as much as I did! Oh, and it doesn't hurt that it all takes place in beautiful Tuscany. Thanks to the Mills & Boon® editors who put this beautiful continuity together!

Susan Meier

A BRIDE FOR THE ITALIAN BOSS

BY
SUSAN MEIER

MILLS & BOON

First published in Great Britain 2015
by Mills & Boon, an imprint of Harlequin (UK) Limited,
Eton House, 18-24 Paradise Road, Richmond, Surrey, TW9 1SR

© 2015 Harlequin Books S.A.

Special thanks and acknowledgement are given to Susan Meier
for her contribution to *The Vineyards of Calanetti* series

ISBN: 978-0-263-25836-3

Harlequin (UK) Limited's policy is to use papers that are natural,
renewable and recyclable products and made from wood grown in
sustainable forests. The logging and manufacturing processes conform
to the legal environmental regulations of the country of origin.

Printed and bound in Great Britain
by CPI Antony Rowe, Chippenham, Wiltshire

Susan Meier is the author of over fifty books for Mills & Boon®. *The Tycoon's Secret Daughter* was a RITA® Award finalist and *Nanny for the Millionaire's Twins* won the Book Buyers' Best award and was a finalist in the National Readers' Choice awards. She is married and has three children. One of eleven children herself, she loves to write about the complexity of families and totally believes in the power of love.

Visit the author profile page at millsandboon.co.uk for more titles

I want to thank the lovely editors at Mills & Boon®
for creating such a great continuity!
Everyone involved LOVED this idea. Thank you!

CHAPTER ONE

ITALY HAD TO BE the most beautiful place in the world.

Daniella Tate glanced around in awe at the cobblestone streets and blue skies of Florence. She'd taken a train here, but now had to board a bus for the village of Monte Calanetti.

After purchasing her ticket, she strolled to a wooden bench. But as she sat, she noticed a woman a few rows over, with white-blond hair and a slim build. The woman stared out into space; the faraway look in her eyes triggered Daniella's empathy. Having grown up a foster child, she knew what it felt like to be alone, sometimes scared, usually confused. And she saw all three of those emotions in the woman's pretty blue eyes.

An announcement for boarding the next bus came over the public address system. An older woman sitting beside the blonde rose and slid her fingers around the bag sitting at her feet. The pretty blonde rose, too.

"Excuse me. That's my bag."

The older woman spoke in angry, rapid-fire Italian and the blonde, speaking American English, said, "I'm sorry. I don't understand a word of what you're saying."

But the older woman clutched the bag to her and very clearly told the American that it was her carry-on.

Daniella bounced from her seat and scurried over. She faced the American. "I speak Italian, perhaps I can help?"

Then she turned to the older woman. In flawless Italian, she asked if she was sure the black bag was hers, because there was a similar bag on the floor on the other side.

The older woman flushed with embarrassment. She apologetically gave the bag to the American, grabbed her carry-on and scampered off to catch her bus.

The pretty blonde sighed with relief and turned her blue eyes to Daniella. "Thank you."

"No problem. When you responded in English it wasn't a great leap to assume you didn't speak the language."

The woman's eyes clouded. "I don't."

"Do you have a friend coming to meet you?"

"No."

Dani winced. "Then I hope you have a good English-to-Italian dictionary."

The American pointed to a small listening device. "I've downloaded the 'best' language system." She smiled slightly. "It promises I'll be fluent in five weeks."

Dani laughed. "It could be a long five weeks." She smiled and offered her hand. "I'm Daniella, by the way."

The pretty American hesitated, but finally shook Daniella's hand and said, "Louisa."

"It's my first trip to Italy. I've been teaching English in Rome, but my foster mother was from Tuscany. I'm going to use this final month of my trip to find her home."

Louisa tilted her head. "Your foster mother?"

Dani winced. "Sorry. I'm oversharing."

Louisa smiled.

"It's just that I'm so excited to be here. I've always wanted to visit Italy." She didn't mention that her long-time boyfriend had proposed the day before she left for her teaching post in Rome. That truly would be oversharing, but also she hadn't known what to make of Paul's request to marry him. Had he proposed before her trip to tie her to him? Or had they hit the place in their relationship where marriage really was the next step? Were they ready? Was marriage right for them?

Too many questions came with his offer of marriage. So she hadn't accepted. She'd told him she would answer him when she returned from Italy. She'd planned this February side trip to be a nice, uncomplicated space of time before she settled down to life as a teacher in the New York City school system. Paul had ruined it with a proposal she should have eagerly accepted, but had stumbled over. So her best option was not to think about it until she had to.

Next month.

"I extended my trip so I could have some time to bum around. See the village my foster mother came from, and hopefully meet her family."

To Daniella's surprise, Louisa laughed. "That sounds like fun."

The understanding in Louisa's voice caused Danielle to brighten again, thinking they had something in common. "So you're a tourist, too?"

"No."

Dani frowned. Louisa's tone in that one simple word suddenly made her feel as if she'd crossed a line. "I'm sorry. I don't mean to pry."

Louisa sighed. "It's okay. I'm just a bit nervous. You were kind to come to my rescue. I don't mean to be such a ninny. I'm on my way to Monte Calanetti."

Daniella's mouth fell open. "So am I."

The announcement that their bus was boarding came over the loudspeaker. Danielle faced the gate. Louisa did, too.

Dani smiled. "Looks like we're off."

"Yes." Louisa's mysterious smile formed again.

They boarded the bus and Daniella chose a spot in the middle, believing that was the best place to see the sights on the drive to the quaint village. After tucking her backpack away, she took her seat.

To her surprise, Louisa paused beside her. "Do you mind if I sit with you?"

Daniella happily said, "Of course, I don't mind! That would be great."

But as Louisa sat, Daniella took note again that something seemed off about her. Everything Louisa did had a sense of hesitancy about it. Everything she said seemed incomplete.

"So you have a month before you go home?"

"All of February." Daniella took a deep breath. "And I intend to enjoy every minute of it. Even if I do have to find work."

"Work?"

"A waitressing job. Or maybe part-time shop clerk. That kind of thing. New York is a very expensive place to live. I don't want to blow every cent I made teaching on a vacation. I'll need that money when I get back home. So I intend to earn my spending money while I see the sights."

As the bus eased out of the station, Louisa said, "That's smart."

Dani sat up, not wanting to miss anything. Louisa laughed. "Your foster mother should have come with you."

Pain squeezed Daniella's heart. Just when she thought she was adjusted to her loss, the reality would swoop in and remind her that the sweet, loving woman who'd saved her was gone. She swallowed hard. "She passed a few months ago. She left me the money for my plane ticket to Italy in her will."

Louisa's beautiful face blossomed with sympathy. "I'm so sorry. That was careless of me."

Daniella shook her head. "No. You had no way of knowing."

Louisa studied her. "So you have no set plans? No schedule of things you want to see and do? No places you've already scouted out to potentially get a job?"

"No schedule. I want to wing it. I've done a bit of research about Rosa's family and I know the language. So I think I'll be okay."

Louisa laughed. "Better off than I'll be since I don't know the language." She held up her listening device. "At least not for another five weeks."

The bus made several slow turns, getting them out of the station and onto the street.

Taking a final look at Florence, Dani breathed, "Isn't this whole country gorgeous?" Even in winter with barren trees, the scene was idyllic. Blue skies. Rolling hills.

"Yes." Louisa bit her lip, then hesitantly said, "I'm here because I inherited something, too."

"Really?"

"Yes." She paused, studied Daniella's face as if assessing if she could trust her before continuing, "A villa."

"Oh, my God! A *villa*!"

Louisa glanced away. "I know. It's pretty amazing. The place is called Palazzo di Comparino."

"Do you have pictures?"

"Yes." She pulled out a picture of a tall, graceful house. Rich green vines grew in rows in the background beneath a blue sky.

It was everything Dani could do not to gape in awe. "It's beautiful."

Louisa laughed. "Yes. But so far I haven't seen anything in Italy that isn't gorgeous." She winced. "I hate to admit it, but I'm excited."

"I'd be beyond excited."

"I'm told Monte Calanetti developed around Palazzo Chianti because of the vineyard which is part of the villa I inherited. Back then, they would have needed lots of help picking grapes, making the wine. Those people are the ancestors of the people who live there now."

"That is so cool."

"Yes, except I know nothing about running a vineyard."

Daniella batted a hand. "With the internet these days, you can learn anything."

Louisa sucked in a breath. "I hope so."

Daniella laid her hand on Louisa's in a show of encouragement. "You'll be fine."

Louise's face formed another of her enigmatic smiles and Daniella's sixth sense perked up again. Louisa appeared to want to be happy, but behind her smile was something...

Louisa brought her gaze back to Daniella's. "You know, I could probably use a little help when I get there."

"Help?"

"I don't think I'm just going to move into a villa without somebody coming to question me."

"Ah."

"And I'm going to be at a loss if they're speaking Italian."

Dani winced. "Especially if it's the sheriff."

Louisa laughed. "I don't even know if they have sheriffs here. My letter is in English, but the officials are probably Italian. It could turn out to be a mess. So, I'd be happy to put you up for a while." She caught Dani's gaze. "Even all four weeks you're looking for your foster mom's relatives— if you'd be my translator."

Overwhelmed by the generous offer, Daniella said, "That would be fantastic. But I wouldn't want to put you out."

"You'll certainly earn your keep if somebody comes to check my story."

Daniella grinned. "I'd be staying in a villa."

Louisa laughed. "I *own* a villa."

"Okay, then. I'd be happy to be your translator while I'm here."

"Thank you."

Glad for the friendship forming between them, Daniella engaged Louisa in conversation as miles of hills and blue, blue sky rolled past them. Then suddenly a walled village appeared to the right. The bus turned in.

Aged, but well-maintained stucco, brick and stone buildings greeted them. Cobblestone streets were filled with happy, chatting people. Through the large front windows of the establishments, Dani could see the coffee drinkers or diners inside while outdoor dining areas sat empty because of the chilly temperatures.

The center circle of the town came into view. The bus made the wide turn but Dani suddenly saw a sign that read Palazzo di Comparino. The old, worn wood planks had a thick black line painted through them as if to cancel out the offer of vineyard tours.

Daniella grabbed Louisa's arm and pointed out the window. "Look!"

"Oh, my gosh!" Louisa jumped out of her seat and yelled, "Stop!"

Daniella rose, too. She said, *"Fermi qui, per favore."*

It took a minute for the bus driver to hear and finally halt the bus. After gathering their belongings, Louisa and Daniella faced the lane that led to Louisa's villa. Because Dani had only a backpack and Louisa had two suitcases and a carry-on bag, Daniella said, "Let me take your suitcase."

Louisa smiled. "Having you around is turning out to be very handy."

Daniella laughed as they walked down the long lane that took them to the villa. The pale brown brick house soon became visible. The closer they got, the bigger it seemed to be.

Louisa reverently whispered, "Holy cow."

Daniella licked her suddenly dry lips. "It's huge."

The main house sprawled before them. Several stories tall, and long and deep, like a house with suites not bedrooms, Louisa's new home could only be described as a mansion.

They silently walked up the stone path to the front door. When they reached it, Louisa pulled out a key and manipulated the lock. As the door opened, the stale, musty scent of a building that had been locked up for years assaulted them. Dust and cobwebs covered the crystal chandelier in the huge marble-floored foyer as well as the paintings on the walls and the curved stairway.

Daniella cautiously stepped inside. "Is your family royalty?"

Louisa gazed around in awe. "I didn't think so."

"Meaning they could be?"

"I don't know." Louisa turned to the right and walked into a sitting room. Again, dust covered everything. A teacup sat on a table by a dusty chair. Passing through that room, they entered another that appeared to be a library or study. From there, they found a dining room.

Watermarks on the ceiling spoke of damage from a second-floor bathroom or maybe even the roof. The kitchen was old and in need of remodeling. The first-floor bathrooms were outdated, as was every bathroom in the suites upstairs.

After only getting as far as the second floor, Louisa turned to Daniella with tears in her eyes. "I'm so sorry. I didn't realize the house would be in such disrepair. From the picture, it looked perfect. If you want to get a hotel room in town, I'll understand."

"Are you kidding?" Daniella rolled Louisa's big suitcase to a stop and walked into the incredibly dusty, cobweb-covered bedroom. She spun around and faced Louisa. "I love it. With a dust rag, some cleanser for the bathroom and a window washing, this room will be perfect."

Louisa hesitantly followed Daniella into the bedroom. "You're an optimist."

Daniella laughed. "I didn't say you wouldn't need to call a contractor about a few things. But we can clean our rooms and the kitchen."

Raffaele Mancini stared at Gino Scarpetti, a tall, stiff man, who worked as the maître d' for Mancini's, Rafe's very exclusive, upscale, Michelin-starred restaurant located in the heart of wine country.

Mancini's had been carefully crafted to charm customers. The stone and wood walls of the renovated farmhouse gave the place the feel of days long gone. Shutters on the windows blocked the light of the evening sun, but also added to the Old World charisma. Rows of bottles of Merlot and Chianti reminded diners that this area was the home of the best vineyards, the finest wines.

Gino ripped off the Mancini's name tag pinned to his white shirt. "You, sir, are now without a maître d'."

A hush fell over the dining room. Even the usual clink and clatter of silverware and the tinkle of good crystal wineglasses halted.

Gino slapped the name tag into Rafe's hand. Before Rafe could comment or argue, the man was out the door.

Someone began to clap. Then another person. And another. Within seconds the sophisticated Tuscany restaurant dining room filled with the sounds of applause and laughter.

Laughter!

They were enjoying his misery!

He looked at the line of customers forming beside the podium just inside the door, then the chattering diners laughing about his temper and his inability to keep good help. He tossed his hands in the air before he marched back to the big ultramodern stainless-steel restaurant kitchen.

"You!"

He pointed at the thin boy who'd begun apprenticing at Mancini's the week before. "Take off your smock and get to the maître d' stand. You are seating people."

The boy's brown eyes grew round with fear. "I...I..."

Rafe raised a brow. "You can't take names and seat customers?"

"I can..."

"But you don't want to." Rafe didn't have to say anything beyond that. He didn't need to say, "If you can't obey orders, you're fired." He didn't need to remind anyone in *his* kitchen that he was boss or that anyone working in the restaurant needed to be able to do *anything* that needed to be done to assure the absolute best dining experience for the customers. Everyone knew he was not a chef to be trifled with.

Except right now, in the dining room, they were laughing at him.

The boy whipped off his smock, threw it to a laundry bin and headed out to the dining room.

Seeing the white-smocked staff gaping at him, Rafe shook his head. "Get to work!"

Knives instantly rose. The clatter of chopping and the sizzle of sautéing filled the kitchen.

He sucked in a breath. Not only was his restaurant plagued by troubles, but now it seemed the diners had no sympathy.

"You shouldn't have fired Gino." Emory Danoto, Rafe's sous-chef, spoke as he worked. Short and bald with a happy face and nearly as much talent as Rafe in the kitchen, Emory was also Rafe's mentor.

Rafe glanced around, inspecting the food prep, pretending he was fine. Damn it. He *was* fine. He did not want a frightened rabbit working for him. Not even outside the kitchen. And the response of the diners? That was a fluke. Somebody apparently believed it was funny to see a world-renowned chef tortured by incompetents.

"I didn't fire Gino. He quit."

Emory cast him a condemning look. "You yelled at him."

Rafe yelled, "I yell at everybody." Then he calmed himself and shook his head. "I am the chef. I *am* Mancini's."

"And you must be obeyed."

"Don't make me sound like a prima donna. I am doing what's best for the restaurant."

"Well, Mr. I'm-Doing-What's-Best-for-the-Restaurant, have you forgotten about our upcoming visit from the Michelin people?"

"A rumor."

Emory sniffed a laugh. "Since when have we ever ignored a rumor that we were to be visited? Your star rating could be in jeopardy. You're the one who says chefs who ignore rumors get caught with their pants down. If we want to keep our stars, we have to be ready for this visit."

Rafe stifled a sigh. Emory was right, of course. His trusted friend only reminded him of what he already knew. Having located his business in the countryside, instead of in town, he'd made it even more exclusive. But that also meant he didn't get street traffic. He needed word of mouth. He needed every diner to recommend him to their friends. He needed to be in travel brochures. To be a stop for tour buses. To be recommended by travel agents. He couldn't lose a star.

The lunch crowd left. Day quickly became night. Before Rafe could draw a steady breath the restaurant filled again. Wasn't that the way of it when everything was falling apart around you? With work to be done, there was no time to think things through. When the last patron finally departed and the staff dispersed after the kitchen cleaning, Rafe walked behind the shiny wood bar, pulled a bottle of whiskey from the shelf, along with a glass, and slid onto a tall, black, wrought iron stool.

Hearing the sound of the door opening, he yelled, "We're closed." Then grimaced. Was he trying to get a reputation for being grouchy rather than exacting?

"Good thing I'm not a customer, then."

He swiveled around at the sound of his friend Nico Amatucci's voice.

Tall, dark-haired Nico glanced at the whiskey bottle, then sat on a stool beside Rafe. "Is there a reason you're drinking alone?"

Rafe rose, got another glass and set it on the bar. He poured whiskey into the glass and slid it to Nico. "I'm not drinking alone."

"But you were going to."

"I lost my maître d'."

Nico raised his glass in salute and drank the shot. "You're surprised?"

"I'm an artist."

"You're a pain in the ass."

"That, too." He sighed. "But I don't want to be. I just want things done correctly. I'll spread the word tomorrow that I'm looking for someone. Not a big deal." He made the statement casually, but deep down he knew he was wrong. It was a big deal. "Oh, who am I kidding? I don't have the week or two it'll take to collect résumés and interview people. I need somebody tomorrow."

Nico raised his glass to toast. "Then, you, my friend, are in trouble."

Didn't Rafe know it.

CHAPTER TWO

THE NEXT MORNING, Daniella and Louisa found a tin of tea and some frozen waffles in a freezer. "We're so lucky no one had the electricity shut off."

"Not lucky. The place runs off a generator. We turn it on in winter to keep the pipes from freezing."

Daniella and Louisa gasped and spun around at the male voice behind them.

A handsome dark-haired man stood in the kitchen doorway, frowning at them. Though he appeared to be Italian, he spoke flawless English. "I'm going to have to ask you to leave. I'll let you finish your breakfast, but this is private property."

Louisa's chin lifted. "I know it's private property. I'm Louisa Harrison. I inherited this villa."

The man's dark eyes narrowed. "I don't suppose you have proof of that?"

"Actually, I do. A letter from my solicitor." She straightened her shoulders. "I think the better question is, who are you?"

"I'm Nico Amatucci." He pointed behind him. "I live next door. I've been watching over this place." He smiled thinly. "I'd like to see the letter from your solicitor. Or—" he pulled out his cell phone "—should I call the police?"

Louisa brushed her hands down her blue jeans to remove the dust they'd collected when she and Daniella had searched for tea. "No need."

Not wanting any part of the discussion, Daniella began preparing the tea.

"And who are you?"

She shrugged. "Just a friend of Louisa's."

He sniffed as if he didn't believe her. Not accustomed to being under such scrutiny, Daniella focused all her attention on getting water into the teapot.

Louisa returned with the letter. When Nico reached for it, she held it back. "Not so fast. I'll need the key you used to get in."

He held Louisa's gaze. Even from across the room, Daniella felt the heat of it.

"Only if your papers check out." His frosty smile could have frozen water. "Palazzo di Comparino has been empty for years. Yet, suddenly here you are."

"With a letter," she said, handing it to Nico.

He didn't release her gaze as he took the letter from her hands, and then he scanned it and peered at Louisa again. "Welcome to Palazzo di Comparino."

Daniella let out her pent-up breath.

Louisa held his gaze. "Just like that? How do you know I didn't fake this letter?"

Giving the paper back to her, he said, "First, I knew the name of the solicitor handling the estate. Second, there are a couple of details in the letter that an outsider wouldn't know. You're legit."

Though Daniella would have loved to have known the details, Louisa didn't even seem slightly curious. She tucked the sheet of paper into her jeans pocket.

Nico handed his key to Louisa as he glanced around the kitchen. "Being empty so long, the place is in disrepair. So if there's anything I can do to help—"

Louisa cut him off with a curt "I'm fine."

Nico's eyes narrowed. Daniella didn't know if he was

unaccustomed to his offers of assistance being ignored, or if something else was happening here, but the kitchen became awkwardly quiet.

When Daniella's teapot whistled, her heart jumped. Always polite, she asked, "Can I get anyone tea?"

Watching Louisa warily, Nico said, "I'd love a cup."

Drat. He was staying. Darn the sense of etiquette her foster mother had drilled into her.

"I'll make some later," Louisa said as she turned and walked out of the kitchen, presumably to put the letter and the key away.

As the door swung closed behind her, Nico said, "She's a friendly one."

Daniella winced. She'd like to point out to Mr. Nico Amatucci that he'd been a tad rude when he'd demanded to see the letter from the solicitor, but she held her tongue. This argument wasn't any of her business. She had enough troubles of her own.

"Have you known Ms. Harrison long?"

"We just met. I saw someone mistakenly take her bag and helped because Louisa doesn't speak Italian. Then we were on the same bus."

"Oh, so you hit the jackpot when you could find someone to stay with."

Daniella's eyes widened. The man was insufferable. "I'm not taking advantage of her! I just finished a teaching job in Rome. Louisa needs an interpreter for a few weeks." She put her shoulders back. "And today I intend to go into town to look for temporary work to finance a few weeks of sightseeing."

He took the cup of tea from her hands. "What kind of work?"

His softened voice took some of the wind out of her sails. She shrugged. "Anything really. Temp jobs are temp jobs."

"Would you be willing to be a hostess at a restaurant?"

Confused, she said, "Sure."

"I have a friend who needs someone to fill in while he hires a permanent replacement for a maître d' who just quit."

Her feelings for the mysterious Nico warmed a bit. Maybe he wasn't so bad after all? "Sounds perfect."

"Do you have a pen?"

She nodded, pulling one from her purse.

He scribbled down the address on a business card he took from his pocket. "Go here. Don't call. Just go at lunchtime and tell Rafe that Nico sent you." He nodded at the card he'd handed to her. "Show him that and he'll know you're not lying."

He set his tea on the table. "Tell Ms. Harrison I said goodbye."

With that, he left.

Glad he was gone, Daniella glanced at the card in her hands. How could a guy who'd so easily helped her have such a difficult time getting along with Louisa?

She blew her breath out on a long sigh. She supposed it didn't matter. Eventually they'd become friends. They were neighbors after all.

Daniella finished her tea, but Louisa never returned to the kitchen. Excited to tell Louisa of her job prospect, Dani searched the downstairs for her, but didn't find her.

The night before they'd tidied two bedrooms enough that they could sleep in them, so she climbed the stairs and headed for the room Louisa had chosen. She found her new friend wrestling with some bedding.

"What are you doing?"

"I saw a washer and dryer. I thought I'd wash the bedclothes so our rooms really will be habitable tonight."

She raced to help Louisa with the huge comforter. "Our rooms were fine. We don't need these comforters, and the sheets had been protected from the dust by the comforters so they were clean. Besides, these won't fit in a typical washer."

Louisa dropped the comforter. "I know." Her face fell in dismay. "I just need to do something to make the place more livable." Her gaze met Daniella's. "There's dust and clutter…and watermarks that mean some of the bathrooms and maybe even the roof need to be repaired." She sat on the bed. "What am I going to do?"

Dani sat beside her. "We're going to take things one step at a time." She tucked Nico's business card into her pocket. "This morning, we'll clean the kitchen and finish our bedrooms. Tomorrow, we'll pick a room and clean it, and every day after that we'll just keep cleaning one room at a time."

"What about the roof?"

"We'll hope it doesn't rain?"

Louisa laughed. "I'm serious."

"Well, I have a chance for a job at a restaurant."

"You do?"

She smiled. "Yes. Nico knows someone who needs a hostess."

"Oh."

She ignored the dislike in her friend's voice. "What better way to find a good contractor than by chitchatting with the locals?"

Louisa smiled and shook her head. "If anybody can chitchat her way into finding a good contractor, it's you."

"Which is also going to make me a good hostess."

"What time's your appointment?"

"Lunchtime." She winced. "From the address on this card, I think we're going to have to hope there's a car in that big, fancy garage out back."

Standing behind the podium in the entry to Mancini's, Rafe struggled with the urge to throw his hands in the air and storm off. On his left, two American couples spoke broken, ill-attempted Italian in an effort to make reservations for that night. In front of him, a businessman demanded to be seated immediately. To his right, a couple kissed. And behind them, what seemed to be a sea of diners groused and grumbled as he tried to figure out a computer system with a seating chart superimposed with reservations.

How could no one in his kitchen staff be familiar with this computer software?

"Everybody just give me a minute!"

He hit a button and the screen disappeared. After a second of shock, he cursed. He expected the crowd to groan. Instead they laughed. *Laughed. Again, laughter!*

How was it that everybody seemed to be happy that he was suffering? These people—customers—were the people he loved, the people he worked so hard to please. How could they laugh at him?

He tried to get the screen to reappear, but it stayed dark.

"Excuse me. Excuse me. Excuse me."

He glanced up to see an American, clearly forgetting she was in Italy because she spoke English as she made her way through the crowd. Cut in an angled, modern style, her pretty blond hair stopped at her chin. Her blue eyes were determined. The buttons of her black coat had been left open, revealing jeans and pale blue sweater.

When she reached the podium, she didn't even look at Rafe. She addressed the gathered crowd.

"Ladies and gentlemen," she said in flawless Italian. "Give me two minutes and everyone will be seated."

His eyebrows rose. She was a cheeky little thing.

When she finally faced him, her blue eyes locked on his. Rich with color and bright with enthusiasm, they didn't merely display her confidence, they caused his heart to give a little bounce.

She smiled and stuck out her hand. "Daniella Tate. Your friend Nico sent me." When he didn't take her hand, her smile drooped as she tucked a strand of yellow hair behind her ear. But her face brightened again. She rifled in her jeans pocket, pulled out a business card and offered it to him. "See?"

He glanced at Nico's card. "So he believes you are right to be my hostess?"

"Temporarily." She winced. "I just finished a teaching position in Rome. For the next four weeks I'm sightseeing, but I'm trying to supplement my extended stay with a temp job. I think he thinks we can help each other—at least while you interview candidates."

The sweet, melodious tone of her voice caused something warm and soft to thrum through Rafe, something he'd never felt before—undoubtedly relief that his friend had solved his problem.

"I see."

"Hey, buddy, come on. We're hungry! If you're not going to seat us we'll go somewhere else."

Not waiting for him to reply, Daniella nudged Rafe out of the way, stooped down to find a tablet on the maître d' stand shelf and faced the dining area. She quickly drew squares and circles representing all the tables and wrote the number of chairs around each one. She put an X over the tables that were taken.

Had he thought she was cheeky? Apparently that was just the tip of the iceberg.

She faced the Americans. "How many in your party?"

"Four. We want reservations for tonight."

"Time?"

"Seven."

Flipping the tablet page, she wrote their name and the time on the next piece of paper. As the Americans walked out, she said, "Next?"

Awestruck at her audacity, Rafe almost yelled.

Almost.

He could easily give her the boot, but he needed a hostess. He had a growing suspicion about the customers laughing when he lost his temper, as if he was becoming some sort of sideshow. He didn't want his temper to be the reason people came to his restaurant. He wanted his food, the fantastic aromas, the succulent tastes, to be the draw. Wouldn't he be a fool to toss her out?

The businessman pushed his way over to her. "I have an appointment in an hour. I need to be served first."

Daniella Tate smiled at Rafe as if asking permission to seat the businessman, and his brain emptied. She really was as pretty as she was cheeky. Luckily, she took his blank stare as approval. She turned to the businessman and said, "Of course, we'll seat you."

She led the man to the back of the dining room, to a table for two, seated him with a smile and returned to the podium.

Forget about how cheeky she was. Forget about his brain that stalled when he looked at her. She was a very good hostess.

Rafe cleared his throat. "Talk to the waitresses and find out whose turn it is before you seat anyone else." He cleared his throat again. "They have a system."

She smiled at him. "Sure."

His heart did something funny in his chest, forcing his gaze to her pretty blue eyes again. Warmth whooshed through him.

Confused, he turned and marched away. With so much at stake in his restaurant, including, it seemed, his reputation, his funny feelings for an employee were irrelevant. Nothing. Whatever trickled through his bloodstream, it had to be more annoyance than attraction. After all, recommendation from Nico or not, she'd sort of walked in and taken over his restaurant.

Dani stared after the chef as he left. She wasn't expecting someone so young…or so gorgeous. At least six feet tall, with wavy brown hair so long he had it tied off his face and gray eyes, the guy could be a celebrity chef on television back home. Just looking at him had caused her breathing to stutter. She actually felt a rush of heat career through her veins. He was *that* good-looking.

But it was also clear that he was in over his head without a maître d'. As she'd stood in the back of the long line to get into the restaurant, her good old-fashioned American common sense had kicked in, and she'd simply done what needed to be done: pushed her way to the front, grabbed some menus and seated customers. And he'd hired her.

Behind her someone said, "You'd better keep your hair behind your ears. He'll yell about it being in your face and potentially in his food once he gets over being happy you're here."

She turned to see one of the waitresses. Dressed in black trousers and a white blouse, she looked slim and professional.

"*That* was happy?"

Her pretty black ponytail bobbed as she nodded. "*Sì.* That was happy."

"Well, I'm going to hate seeing him upset."

"Prepare yourself for it. Because he gets upset every day. Several times a day. That's why Gino quit. I'm Allegra, by the way. The other two waitresses are Zola and Giovanna. And the chef is Chef Mancini. Everyone calls him Chef Rafe."

"He said you have a system of how you want people seated?"

Allegra took Daniella's seating chart and drew two lines dividing the tables into three sections. "Those are our stations. You seat one person in mine, one person in Zola's and one person in Gio's, then start all over again."

Daniella smiled. "Easy-peasy."

"*Scusi?*"

"That means 'no problem.'"

"Ah. *Sì.*" Allegra smiled and walked away. Daniella took two more menus and seated another couple.

The lunchtime crowd that had assembled at the door of

Mancini's settled quickly. Dani easily found a rhythm of dividing the customers up between the three waitresses. Zola and Gio introduced themselves, and she actually had a good time being hostess of the restaurant that looked like an Old World farmhouse and smelled like pure heaven. The aromas of onions and garlic, sweet peppers and spicy meats rolled through the air, making her confident she could talk up the food and promise diners a wonderful meal, even without having tasted it.

During the lull after lunch, Zola and Gio went home. The dining room grew quiet. Not sure if she should stay or leave, since Allegra remained to be available for the occasional tourist who ambled in, Daniella stayed, too.

In between customers, she helped clear and reset tables, checked silverware to make sure it sparkled, arranged chairs so that everything in the dining room was picture-perfect.

But soon even the stragglers stopped. Daniella stood by the podium, her elbow leaning against it, her chin on her closed fist, wondering what Louisa was doing.

"Why are you still here?"

The sound of Rafe's voice sent a surge of electricity through her.

She turned with a gasp. Her voice wobbled when she said, "I thought you'd need me for dinner."

"You were supposed to go home for the break. Or are you sneakily trying to get paid for hours you really don't work?"

Her eyes widened. Anger punched through her. What the hell was wrong with this guy? She'd done him a favor and he was questioning her motives?

Without thinking, she stormed over to him. Putting herself in his personal space, she looked up and caught his gaze. "And how was I supposed to know that, since you didn't tell me?"

She expected him to back down. At the very least to realize his mistake. Instead, he scoffed. "It's common sense."

"Well, in America—"

He cut her off with a harsh laugh. "You Americans. Think you know everything. But you're not in America now. You are in Italy." He pointed a finger at her nose. "You will do what I say."

"Well, I'll be happy to do what you say as soon as you say something!"

Allegra stopped dropping silverware onto linen-covered tables. The empty, quiet restaurant grew stone-cold silent. Time seemed to crawl to a stop. The vein in Rafe's temple pulsed.

Dani's body tingled. Every employee in the world knew it wasn't wise to yell at the boss, but, technically, she wasn't yelling. She was standing up to him. As a foster child, she'd had to learn how to protect herself, when to stay quiet and when to demand her rights. If she let him push her around now, he'd push her around the entire month she worked for him.

He threw his hands in the air, pivoted away from her and headed to the kitchen. "Go the hell home and come back for dinner."

Daniella blew out the breath she'd been holding. Her heart pounded so hard it hurt, but the tingling in her blood became a surge of power. He might not have said the words, but she'd won that little battle of wills.

Still, she felt odd that their communication had come down to a sort of yelling match and knew she had to get the heck out of there.

She grabbed her purse and headed for the old green car she and Louisa had found in the garage.

Ten minutes later, she was back in the kitchen of Palazzo di Comparino.

Though Louisa had sympathetically made her a cup of tea, she laughed when Daniella told her the story.

"It's not funny," Dani insisted, but her lips rose into a smile when she thought about how she must have looked standing up to the big bad chef everybody seemed to be afraid of. She wouldn't tell her new friend that standing up to him had put fire in her blood and made her heart gallop like a prize stallion. She didn't know what that was all about, but she did know part of it, at least, stemmed from how good-looking he was.

"Okay. It was a little funny. But I like this job. It would be great to keep it for the four weeks I'm here. But he didn't tell me what time I was supposed to go back. So we're probably going to get into another fight."

"Or you could just go back at six. If he yells that you're late, calmly remind him that he didn't give you the time you were to return. Make it his fault."

"It is his fault."

Louisa beamed. "Exactly. If you don't stand up to him now, you'll either lose the job or spend the weeks you work for him under his thumb. You have to do this."

Dani sighed. "That's what I thought."

Taking Louisa's advice, she returned to the restaurant at six. A very small crowd had built by the maître d' podium, and when she entered, she noticed that most of the tables weren't filled. Rafe shoved a stack of menus at her and walked away.

She shook her head, but smiled at the next customers in line. He might have left without a word, but he hadn't engaged her in a fight and it appeared she still had her job.

Maybe the answer to this was to just stay out of his way?

The evening went smoothly. Again, the wonderful scents that filled the air prompted her to talk up the food, the waitstaff and the wine.

After an hour or so, Rafe called her into the kitchen. Absolutely positive he had nothing to yell at her about, she straightened her shoulders and walked into the stainless-steel room and over to the stove where he stood.

"You wanted to see me?"

He presented a fork filled with pasta to her. "This is my signature ravioli. I hear you talking about my dishes, so I want you to taste so you can honestly tell customers it is the best food you have ever eaten."

She swallowed back a laugh at his confidence, but when her lips wrapped around the fork and the flavor of the sweet sauce exploded on her tongue, she pulled the ravioli off the fork and into her mouth with a groan. "Oh, my God."

"It is perfect, *si*?"

"You're right. It is probably the best food I've ever eaten."

Emory, the short, bald sous-chef, scrambled over. "Try this." He raised a fork full of meat to her lips.

She took the bite and again, she groaned. "What is that?"

"Beef *brasato*."

"Oh, my God, that's good."

A younger chef suddenly appeared before her with a spoon of soup. "Minestrone," he said, holding the spoon out to her.

She drank the soup and closed her eyes to savor. "You guys are the best cooks in the world."

Everyone in the kitchen stopped. The room fell silent.

But Emory laughed. "Chef Rafe is *one* of the best chefs in the world. These are his recipes."

She turned and smiled at Rafe. "You're amazing."

She'd meant his cooking was amazing. His recipes were amazing. Or maybe the way he could get the best out of his staff was amazing. But saying the words while looking into his silver-gray eyes, the simple sentence took on a totally different meaning.

The room grew quiet again. She felt her face reddening. Rafe held her gaze for a good twenty seconds before he finally pointed at the door. "Go tell that to customers."

She walked out of the kitchen, licking the remains of the fantastic food off her lips as she headed for the podium.

With the exception of that crazy little minute of eye contact, tasting the food had been fun. She loved how proud the entire kitchen staff seemed to be of the delicious dishes they prepared. And she saw the respect they had for their boss. Chef Rafe. Clearly a very talented man.

With two groups waiting to be seated, she grabbed menus and walked the first couple to a table. "Right this way."

"Any specialties tonight?"

She faced the man and woman behind her, saying, "I can honestly recommend the chef's signature ravioli." With the taste of the food still on her tongue, she smiled. "And the minestrone soup is to die for. But if you're in the mood for beef, there's a beef *brasato* that you'll never forget."

She said the words casually, but sampling the food had had the oddest effect on her. Suddenly she felt part of it. She didn't merely feel like a good hostess who could recommend the delicious dishes because she'd tasted them. She got an overwhelming sense that she was meant to be here. The feeling of destiny was so strong it nearly overwhelmed her. But she drew in a quiet breath, smiled at the couple and seated them.

Sense of destiny? That was almost funny. Children who grew up in foster care gave up on destiny early, and contented themselves with a sense of worth, confidence. It was better to educate yourself to be employable than to dally in daydreams.

As the night went on, Rafe and his staff continued to give her bites and tastes of the dishes they prepared. As she became familiar with the items on the menu, she tempted guests to try things. But she also listened to stories of the sights the tourists had seen that day, and soothed the egos of those who spoke broken Italian by telling stories of teaching English as a second language in Rome.

And the feeling that she was meant to be there grew, until her heart swelled with it.

* * *

Rafe watched her from the kitchen door. Behind him, Emory laughed. "She's pretty, right?"

Rafe faced him, concerned that his friend had seen their thirty seconds of eye contact over the ravioli and recognized that Rafe was having trouble seeing Daniella Tate as an employee because she was so beautiful. When she'd called him amazing, he'd struggled to keep his gaze off her lips, but that didn't stop the urge to kiss her. It blossomed to life in his chest and clutched the air going into and out of his lungs, making them stutter. He'd needed all of those thirty seconds to get ahold of himself.

But Emory's round face wore his usual smile. Nothing out of the ordinary. No light of recognition in his eyes. Rafe's unexpected reactions hadn't been noticed.

Rafe turned back to the crack between the doors again. "She's chatty."

"You did tell her to talk up the food." Emory sidled up to the slim opening. "Besides, the customers seem to love her."

"Bah!" He spun away from the door. "We don't need for customers to love her. They come here for the food."

Emory shrugged. "Maybe. But we're both aware Mancini's was getting to be a little more well-known for your temper than for its meals. A little attention from a pretty girl talking up *your* dishes might just cure your reputation problem. Put the food back in the spotlight instead of your temper."

"I still think she talks too much."

Emory shook his head. "Suit yourself."

Rafe crossed his arms on his chest. He would suit himself. He was *famous* for suiting himself. That was how he'd gotten to be a great chef. By learning and testing until he created great meals. And he wanted the focus on those meals.

The first chance he got, he intended to have a talk with Daniella Tate.

CHAPTER THREE

AT THE END of the night, when the prep tables were spotless, the kitchen staff raced out the back door. Rafe ambled into the dining room as the waitresses headed for the front door, Daniella in their ranks.

Stopping behind the bar, he called, "No. No. You…Daniella. You and I need to talk."

Her steps faltered and she paused. Eventually, she turned around. "Sure. Great."

Allegra and Gio tossed looks of sympathy at her as the door closed softly behind them.

Her shoulders straightened and she walked over to him. "What is it?"

"You are chatty."

She burst out laughing. "I know." As comfortable as an old friend, she slid onto a bar stool across from him. "Got myself into a lot of trouble in school for that."

"Then you will not be offended if I ask you to project a more professional demeanor with the customers?"

"Heck, no. I'm not offended. I think you're crazy for telling me not to be friendly. But I'm not offended."

Heat surged through Rafe's blood, the way it had when she'd nibbled the ravioli from his fork and called him amazing. But this time he was prepared for it. He didn't know what it was about this woman that got him going, why their arguments fired his blood and their pleasant encounters made him want to kiss her, but he did know he had to control it.

He pulled a bottle of wine from the rack beneath the bar and poured two glasses. Handing one of the glasses to her, he asked, "Do you think it's funny to argue with your boss?"

"I'm not arguing with you. I'm giving you my opinion."

He stayed behind the bar, across from her so he could see her face, her expressive blue eyes. "Ah. So, now I understand. You believe you have a right to an opinion."

She took a sip of the wine. "Maybe not a right. But it's kind of hard not to have an opinion."

He leaned against the smooth wooden surface between them, unintentionally getting closer, then finding that he liked it there because he could smell the hint of her perfume or shampoo. "Perhaps. But a smart employee learns to stifle them."

"As you said, I'm chatty."

"Do it anyway."

She sucked in a breath, pulling back slightly as if trying to put space between them. "Okay."

He laughed. "Okay? My chatty hostess is just saying okay?"

"It's your restaurant."

He saluted her with his wineglass. "At least we agree on something."

But when she set her glass on the bar, slid off the stool and headed for the door, his heart sank.

He shook his head, grabbed the open bottle of wine and went in the other direction, walking toward the kitchen where he would check the next day's menu. It was silly, foolish to be disappointed she was leaving. Not only did he barely know the woman, but he wasn't in the market for a girlfriend. His instincts might be thinking of things like kissing, but he hadn't dated in four years. He had affairs and one-night stands. And a smart employer didn't have a one-night stand with an employee. Unless he wanted trouble. And he did not.

He'd already had one relationship that had almost destroyed his dream. He'd fallen so hard for Kamila Troccoli that when she wasn't able to handle the demands of his schedule, he'd pared it back. Desperate to keep her, he'd refused plum apprenticeships, basically giving up his goal of being a master chef and owning a chain of restaurants.

But she'd left him anyway. After a year of building his life around her, he'd awakened one morning to find she'd simply gone. It had taken four weeks before he could go back to work, but his broken heart hadn't healed until he'd realized relationships were for other men. He had a dream that a romance had nearly stolen from him. A wise man didn't forget hard lessons, or throw them away because of a pretty girl.

Almost at the kitchen door, he stopped. "And, Daniella?"

She faced him.

"No jeans tomorrow. Black trousers and a white shirt."

Daniella raced to her car, her heart thumping in her chest. Having Rafe lean across the bar, so close to her, had been the oddest thing. Her blood pressure had risen. Her breathing had gone funny. And damned if she didn't want to run her fingers through his wavy hair. Unbound, it had fallen to his shoulders, giving him the look of a sexy pirate.

The desire to touch him had been so strong, she would have agreed to anything to be able to get away from him so she could sort this out.

And just when she'd thought she was free, he'd said her name. *Daniella.* The way it had rolled off his tongue had been so sexy, she'd shuddered.

Calling herself every kind of crazy, she got into Louisa's old car and headed home. A mile up the country road, she pulled through the opening in the stone wall that allowed entry to Monte Calanetti. Driving along the cobblestone street, lit only by streetlights, she marveled at the way her heart warmed at the quaint small town. She'd never felt so at peace as she did in Italy, and she couldn't wait to meet her foster mother's relatives. Positive they'd make a connection, she could see herself coming to Italy every year to visit them.

She followed the curve around the statue in the town square before she made the turn onto the lane for Palazzo di Comparino. She knew Louisa saw only decay and damage when she looked at the crumbling villa, but in her mind's eye Dani could see it as it was in its glory days. Vines heavy with grapes. The compound filled with happy employees. The owner, a proud man.

A lot like Rafe.

She squeezed her eyes shut when the familiar warmth whooshed through her at just the thought of his name. What was it about that guy that got to her? Sure, he was sexy. Really sexy. But she'd met sexy men before. Why did this one affect her like this?

Louisa was asleep, so she didn't have anyone to talk with about her strange feelings. But the next morning over tea, she told Louisa everything that had happened at the restaurant, especially her unwanted urge to touch Rafe when he leaned across the bar and was so close to her, and Louisa—again—laughed.

"This is Italy. Why are you so surprised you're feeling everything a hundred times more passionately?"

Dani's eyes narrowed. Remembering her thoughts about Monte Calanetti, the way she loved the quaint cobblestone streets, the statue fountain in the middle of the square, the happy, bustling people, she realized she did feel everything more powerfully in Italy.

"Do you think that's all it is?"

"Oh, sweetie, this is the land of passion. It's in the air. The water. Something. As long as you recognize what it is, you'll be fine."

"I hope so." She rose from the table. "I also hope there's a thrift shop in town. I have to find black trousers and a white blouse. Rafe doesn't like my jeans."

Louisa laughed as she, too, rose from the table. "I'll bet he likes your jeans just fine."

Daniella frowned.

Louisa slid her arm across her shoulder. "Your butt looks amazing in jeans."

"What does that have to do with anything?"

Louisa gave her a confused look, then shook her head. "Did you ever stop to think that maybe you're *both* reacting extremely to each other. That it's not just you feeling everything, and that's why it's so hard to ignore?"

"You think he's attracted to me?"

"Maybe. Dani, you're pretty and sexy." She laughed. "And Italian men like blondes."

Daniella frowned. "Oh, boy. That just makes things worse."

"Or more fun."

"No! I have a fiancé. Well, not a fiancé. My boyfriend asked me to marry him right before I left."

"You have a boyfriend?"

She winced. "Yeah."

"And he proposed right before you left?"

"Yes."

Louisa sighed. "I guess that rules out an affair with your sexy Italian boss."

Daniella's eyes widened. "I can't have an affair!"

"I know." Louisa laughed. "Come on. Let's go upstairs and see what's in my suitcases. I have to unpack anyway. I'm sure I have black pants and a white shirt."

"Okay."

Glad the subject had changed, Daniella walked with Louisa through the massive downstairs to the masterpiece stairway.

Louisa lovingly caressed the old, worn banister. "I feel

like this should be my first project. Sort of like a symbol that I intend to bring this place back to life."

"Other people might give the kitchen or bathrooms a priority."

Louisa shook her head. "The foyer is the first thing everyone sees when they walk in. I want people to know I'm committed and I'm staying."

"I get it."

It took ten minutes to find the black pants and white shirt in Louisa's suitcase, but Dani remained with Louisa another hour to sort through her clothes and hang them in the closet.

When it was time to leave, she said goodbye to Louisa and headed to the restaurant for the lunch crowd. She stashed her purse on the little shelf of the podium and waited for someone to unlock the door to customers so she could begin seating everyone.

Rafe himself came out. As he walked to the door, his gaze skimmed over her. Pinpricks of awareness rained down on her. Louisa's suggestion that he was attracted to her tiptoed into her brain. What would it be like to have this sexy, passionate man attracted to her?

She shook her head. What the heck was she thinking? He was only looking at her to make sure she had dressed appropriately. He was *not* attracted to her. Good grief. All they ever did was snipe at each other. That was not attraction.

Although, standing up to him did warm her blood…

After opening the door, Rafe strode away without even saying good morning, proving, at least to Dani, that he wasn't attracted to her. As she seated her first customers, he walked to the windows at the back of the old farmhouse and opened the wooden shutters, revealing the picturesque countryside.

The odd feeling of destiny brought Daniella up short again. This time she told herself it was simply an acknowledgment that the day was beautiful, the view perfect. There was no such thing as someone "belonging" somewhere. There was only hard work and planning.

An hour into the lunch shift, a customer called her over and asked to speak with the chef. Fear shuddered through her.

"Rafe?"

The older man nodded. "If he's the chef, yes."

She couldn't even picture the scene if she called Rafe out and this man, a sweet old man with gray hair, blue eyes and a cute little dimple, complained about the food. So she smiled. "Maybe I can help you?"

"Perhaps. But I would like to speak with the chef."

Officially out of options, she smiled and said, "Absolutely."

She turned to find Rafe only a few steps away, his eyes narrowed, his lips thin.

She made her smile as big as she could. "Chef Rafe..." She motioned him over. When he reached her, she politely said, "This gentleman would like to speak with you."

The dining room suddenly grew quiet. It seemed that everyone, including Daniella, held their breath.

Rafe addressed the man. "Yes? What can I do for you? I'm always happy to hear from my customers."

His voice wasn't just calm. It was warm. Dani took a step back. She'd expected him to bark. Instead, he was charming and receptive.

"This is the best ravioli I've ever eaten." The customer smiled broadly. "I wanted to convey my compliments to the chef personally."

Rafe put his hands together as if praying and bowed slightly. *"Grazie."*

"How did you come to pick such a lovely place for a restaurant?"

"The views mostly," Rafe said, smiling, and Dani stared at him. Those crazy feelings rolled through her again.

When it came to his customers he was humble, genuine. And very, very likable.

He turned to her and nodded toward the door. "Customers, Daniella?"

"Yes! Of course!" She pivoted and hurried away to seat the people at the door, her heart thrumming, her nerve endings shimmering. Telling herself she was simply responding to the happy way he chatted with a customer, glad he hadn't yelled at the poor man and glad everything was going so well, she refused to even consider that her appreciation of his good looks was tipping over into a genuine attraction.

She was so busy she didn't hear the rest of Rafe's conversation with the older couple. When they left, Rafe returned to the kitchen and Daniella went about her work. People arrived, she seated them, the staff served them and Rafe milled about the dining room, talking with customers. They gushed over the scene visible through the back windows. And he laughed.

He *laughed*. And the warmth of his love for his customers filled her. But that still didn't mean she was attracted to him. She appreciated him, yes. Respected him? Absolutely. But even though he was gorgeous, she refused to be attracted to him. Except maybe physically…the man *was* gorgeous. And having a boyfriend didn't mean she couldn't *notice* good-looking men… Did it?

When the lunch crowd emptied, and Gio and Zola left, Daniella turned to help Allegra tidy the dining room, but Rafe caught her arm. "Not so fast."

The touch of his hand on her biceps sent electricity straight to her heart. Which speeded up and sent a whoosh of heat through her blood.

Darn it. She *was* attracted to him.

But physically. Just physically.

She turned slowly.

Bright with anger, his gaze bored into her. "What in the hell did you think you were doing?"

With electricity careening through her, she pulled in a shaky breath. "When?"

"When the customer asked to speak with me!" He threw his hands in the air. "Did you think I did not see? I see everything! I heard that man ask to speak with me and heard you suggest that he talk to you."

She sucked in a breath to steady herself. "I was trying to head off a disaster."

"A disaster? He wanted to compliment the chef and you tried to dissuade him. Did you want the compliment for yourself?"

She gasped. "No! I was worried he was going to complain about the food." She took a step closer, now every bit as angry as he was. He was so concerned about his own agenda, he couldn't even tell when somebody was trying to save his sorry butt. "And that you'd scream at him and the whole dining room would hear."

He matched the step she took. "Oh, really? You saw how I spoke to him. I love my customers."

She held her ground. Her gaze narrowed on him. Her heart raced. "Yeah, well I know that now, but I didn't know it when he asked to speak with you."

"You overstepped your boundaries." He took another step, and put them so close her whole body felt energized—

Oh, no.

Now she knew what was going on. She didn't just think Rafe was handsome. She wasn't just *physically* attracted to him. She was completely attracted to him. And she wasn't yelling at him because she was defending herself. She was yelling because it was how he communicated with her. Because he was a stubborn, passionate man, was this how she flirted with him?

Not at all happy with these feelings, she stepped away

from him. Softening her voice, she said, "It won't happen again."

He laughed. "What? You suddenly back down?"

She peered over at him. Why hadn't he simply said, "Thank you," and walked away? That's what he usually did.

Unless Louisa was right and he was attracted to her, too?

The mere thought made her breathless. She sneaked a peek at him—he was distinguished looking with his long hair tied back and his white smock still crisp and clean after hours of work. The memory of his laughter with the customer fluttered through her, stealing her breath again. He was a handsome man, very, very good at what he did and dedicated to his customers. He could have his pick of women. And he was attracted to her?

Preposterous. She didn't for a second believe it, but she was definitely attracted to him. And she was going to have to watch her step.

She cleared her throat. "Unless you want me to hang out until the dinner crowd, I'll be going home now."

He shook his head. "Do not overstep your boundaries again."

She licked her suddenly dry lips. "Oh, believe me, I'll be very, very careful from here on out."

Rafe watched her walk away. His racing heart had stilled. The fire in his blood had fizzled. Disappointment rattled through him. He shook his head and walked back into the kitchen.

"Done yelling at Daniella?"

Rafe scowled at Emory. "She oversteps her place."

"She's trying to keep the peace. To keep the customers happy. And, in case you haven't noticed, they are happy. Today they were particularly happy."

He sniffed in disdain. "I opened the dining room to the view from the back windows."

Emory laughed. "Seriously? You're going with that?"

"All right! So customers like her."

"And no one seems to be hanging around hoping you'll lose your temper."

He scowled.

"She did exactly what we needed to have done. She shifted the temperament in the dining room. Customers are enjoying your food. You should be thrilled to have her around."

Rafe turned away with a "Bah." But deep down inside he *was* thrilled to have her around.

And maybe that wasn't as much of a good thing as Emory thought it was. Because the whole time he was yelling at her, he could also picture himself kissing her.

Worse, the part of him that usually toed the line wasn't behaving. That part kept reminding him she was temporary. She might be an employee, but she wasn't staying forever. He *could* have an affair with this beautiful, passionate woman and not have to worry about repercussions because in a few weeks, she'd be gone. No scene. No broken heart. No expectations. They could have a delicious affair.

CHAPTER FOUR

DANIELLA RETURNED HOME that night exhausted. Louisa hadn't waited up for her, but from the open cabinet doors and trash bags sitting by the door, it was apparent she'd begun cleaning the kitchen.

She dragged herself up the stairs, showered and crawled into bed, refusing to think about the possibility that Rafe might be attracted to her. Not only did she have a marriage proposal waiting at home, but, seriously? Her with Rafe? Mr. Unstable with the former foster child who needed stability? That was insanity.

She woke early the next morning and, after breakfast, she and Louisa loaded outdated food from the pantry into even more trash bags.

Wiping sweat from her brow, Louisa shook her head at the bag of garbage she'd just hauled to the growing pile by the door. "We don't even know what day to set out the trash."

Busy sweeping the now-empty pantry, Dani said, "You could always ask Nico."

Louisa rolled her eyes. "I'm not tromping over to his villa to ask about trash."

"You could call him. I have his card." She frowned. "Or Rafe has his card. I could ask for it back tonight."

"No, thanks. I'll figure this out."

"Or maybe I could ask the girls at the restaurant? Given

that we're so close to Monte Calanetti, one of them probably lives in the village. She'll know what day the trash truck comes by."

Louisa brightened. "Yes. Thank you. That would be great."

But Dani frowned as she swept the last of the dirt onto her dustpan. Louisa's refusal to have anything to do with Nico had gone from unusual to impractical. Still, it wasn't her place to say anything.

She dressed for work in the dark trousers and white shirt Rafe required and drove to the restaurant. Walking in, she noticed that two of the chefs were different, and two of the chefs she was accustomed to seeing weren't there. The same was true in the dining room. Allegra was nowhere to be seen and in her place was a tall, slim waitress named Mila, short for Milana, who told Daniella it was simply Allegra's day off and probably the chefs', too.

"Did you think they'd been fired?" Mila asked with a laugh.

Dani shrugged. "With our boss, you never know."

Mila laughed again. "Only Chef Rafe works twelve hours a day, seven days a week."

"I guess I should ask for a schedule, then."

She turned toward the kitchen but Mila stopped her. "Do yourself a favor and ask Emory about it."

Thinking that sounded like good advice, she nodded and walked into the kitchen. Emory stood at a stainless-steel prep table in the back of the huge, noisy, delicious-smelling room. Grateful that Rafe wasn't anywhere in sight, she approached the sous-chef.

"*Cara!*" he said, opening his arms. "What can I do for you?"

"I was wondering if there was a schedule."

The short, bald man smiled. "Schedule?"

"I'm never really sure when I'm supposed to come in."

"A maître d' works all shifts."

At the sound of Rafe's voice behind her, she winced, sucked in a breath and faced him. "I can't work seven days a week, twelve hours a day. I want this month to do some sightseeing. Otherwise, I could have just gone back to New York City."

He smiled and said, "Ah."

And Daniella's heart about tripped over itself in her chest. He had the most beautiful, sexy smile she had ever seen. Directed at her, it stole her breath, weakened her knees, scared her silly.

"You are correct. Emory will create a schedule."

Surprised at how easy that had been, and not about to hang around when his smile was bringing out feelings she knew were all wrong, she scampered out of the kitchen. Within minutes, Rafe came into the dining room to open Mancini's doors. As he passed her, he smiled at her again.

When he disappeared behind the kitchen doors, she blew out her breath and collapsed against the podium. What was he doing smiling at her? Dear God, was Louisa right? Was he interested in her?

She paused. No. Rafe was too business oriented to be attracted to an employee. This wasn't about attraction. It was about her finally finding her footing with him. He hadn't argued about getting her a schedule. He'd smiled because they were beginning to get along as employer and employee.

Guests began arriving and she went to work. There were enough customers that the restaurant felt busy, but not nearly as busy as they were for dinner. She seated an American couple and walked away but even before she reached the podium, they waved her back.

She smiled. "Having trouble with the Italian?"

The short dark-haired man laughed. "My wife teaches Italian at university. We actually visit every other year. Though this is our first time at Mancini's."

"Well, a very special welcome to you, then. What can I help you with?"

He winced. "Actually, we were kind of hoping to just have soup or a salad, but all you have is a full menu."

"Yes. The chef loves his drama."

The man's wife reached over and touched his arm. "I am sort of hungry for this delicious-sounding spaghetti. Maybe we can eat our big meal now and eat light at dinner."

Her husband laughed. "Fine by me."

Dani waved Gio over to take their orders, but a few minutes later, she had a similar conversation with a group of tourists who had reservations that night at a restaurant in Florence. They'd stopped at Mancini's looking for something light, but Rafe's menu only offered full-course meals.

With the lunchtime crowd thinned and two of the three waitresses gone until dinner, Dani stared at the kitchen door. If she and Rafe really had established a proper working relationship, shouldn't she tell him what customers told her?

Of course, she should. She shouldn't be afraid. She should be a good employee.

She headed for the kitchen. "May I speak with you, Chef Rafe?"

His silver-gray eyes met hers. "Yes?"

She swallowed. It was just plain impossible not to be attracted to this guy. "It's… I… Do you want to hear the things the customers tell me?"

Leaning against his prep table behind him, holding her gaze, he said, "Yes. I always want the opinions of customers."

She drank in a long breath. The soft, seductive tone of his voice, the way he wouldn't release her gaze, all reminded her of Louisa's contention that he was attracted to her. The prospect tied her tongue until she reminded herself that they were at work. And he was dedicated to his diners. In this kitchen, that was all that mattered.

"Okay. Today, I spoke with a couple from the US and a group of tourists, both of whom only wanted soup or salad for lunch."

"We serve soup and salad."

"As part of a meal."

"So they should eat a meal."

"That was actually their point. They didn't want a whole meal. Just soup and salad."

Rafe turned to Emory, his hands raised in question as if he didn't understand what she was saying.

She tried again. "Look. You want people to come in for both lunch and dinner but you only offer dinners on the menu. Who wants a five-course meal for lunch?"

The silver shimmer in Rafe's eyes disappeared and he gaped at her. "Any Italian."

"All right." So much for thinking he was attracted to her. The tone of his voice was now definitely all business and when it came to his business, he was clearly on a different page than she was. But this time she knew she was right. "Maybe Italians do like to eat that way. But half your patrons are tourists. If they want a big meal, they'll come at dinnertime. If they just want to experience the joy that is Mancini's, they'll be here for lunch. And they'll probably only want a salad. Or maybe a burger."

"A burger?" He whispered the word as if it were blasphemy.

"Sure. If they like it, they'll be back for dinner."

The kitchen suddenly got very quiet. Every chef in the room and both busboys had turned to face her.

Rafe quietly said, "This is Italy. Tourists want to experience the culture."

"Yes. You are correct. They do want to experience the culture. But that's only part of why tourists are here. Most tourists don't eat two huge meals a day. It couldn't hurt to put simple salads on the lunch menu, just in case a tourist or two doesn't want to eat five courses."

His gray eyes flared. When he spoke, it was slowly, deliberately. "Miss Daniella, you are a tourist playing hostess. I am a world-renowned chef."

This time the softness of his voice wasn't seductive. It was insulting and her defenses rose. "I know. But I'm the one in the dining room, talking with your customers—"

His eyes narrowed with anger and she stepped back, suddenly wondering what the hell she was doing. He was her boss. As he'd said, a world-renowned chef. Yet here she was questioning him. She couldn't seem to turn off the self-defense mechanisms she'd developed to protect herself in middle school when she was constantly teased about not having a home or questioned because her classmates thought being a foster kid meant she was stupid.

She sucked in a long, shaky breath. "I'm sorry. I don't know why I pushed."

He gave her a nod that more or less dismissed her and she raced out of the kitchen. But two minutes later a customer asked to speak with Rafe. Considering this her opportunity to be respectful to him, so hopefully they could both forget about their soup and salad disagreement, she walked into the kitchen.

But she didn't see Rafe.

She turned to a busboy. "Excuse me. Where's Chef Rafe?"

The young kid pointed at a closed door. "In the office with Emory."

She smiled. "Thanks."

She headed for the door. Just when she would have pushed it open, she heard Emory's voice.

"I'm not entirely sure why you argue with her."

"*I* argue with *her*? I was nothing but nice to that girl and she comes into my kitchen and tells me I don't know my own business."

Dani winced, realizing they were talking about her.

Emory said, "We need her."

And Rafe quickly countered with, "You are wrong. Had Nico not sent her, we would have hired someone else by now. Instead, because Nico told her I was desperate, we're stuck with a woman who thinks we need her, and thinks that gives her the right to make suggestions. Not only do we not need her, but I do not want her here—"

The rest of what Rafe said was lost on Dani as she backed away from the door.

Rafe saying that she wasn't wanted rolled through her, bringing up more of those memories from middle school before she'd found a permanent foster home with Rosa. The feeling of not being wanted, not having a home, rose in her as if she were still that teenage girl who'd been rejected so many times that her scars burrowed the whole way to her soul.

Tears welled in her eyes. But she fought them, telling herself he was right. She shouldn't argue with him. But seriously, this time she'd thought she was giving a valuable suggestion. And she'd stopped when she realized she'd pushed too far.

She just couldn't seem to get her bearings with this guy. And maybe it was time to realize this really wasn't the job for her and leave.

She pivoted away from the door, raced out of the kitchen and over to Gio. "Um, the guy on table three would like to talk with Rafe. Would you mind getting him?"

Gio studied her face, undoubtedly saw the tears shimmering on her eyelids and smiled kindly. "Sure."

Dani walked to the podium, intending to get her purse and her coat to leave, but a customer walked in.

Rafe shook his head as Emory left the office with a laugh. He'd needed to vent and Emory had listened for a few minutes, then he'd shut Rafe down. And that was good. He'd been annoyed that Dani challenged him in front of his staff. But venting to Emory was infinitely better than firing her.

Especially since they did need her. He hadn't even started interviewing for her replacement yet.

He walked into the kitchen at the same time that Gio did. "Chef Rafe, there's a customer who would like to speak with you."

He turned to the sink, rinsed his hands and grabbed his towel, before he motioned for Gio to lead him to the customer.

Stepping into the dining room, he didn't see Dani anywhere, but before he could take that thought any further, he was beside a happy customer who wanted to compliment him on his food.

He listened to the man, scanning the dining room for his hostess. When she finally walked into the dining room from the long hall that led to the restrooms, he sighed with relief. He accepted the praise of his customer, smiled and returned to his work.

An hour later, Dani came into the kitchen. "Chef Mancini, there's a customer who would like to speak with you."

Her voice was soft, meek. She'd also called him Chef Mancini, not Chef Rafe, but he didn't question it. A more businesslike demeanor between them was not a bad thing. Particularly considering that he'd actually wanted to have an affair with her and had been thinking about that all damned day—until they'd gotten into that argument about soup and salad.

Which was why the smile he gave her was nothing but professional. "It would be my pleasure."

He expected her to say, "Thank you." Instead, she nodded, turned and left the kitchen without him.

He rinsed his hands, dried them and headed out to the dining room. She waited by a table in the back. When she saw him she motioned for him to come to the table.

As he walked up, she smiled at the customers. She said, "This is Chef Mancini." Then she strode away.

He happily chatted with the customer for ten minutes, but his gaze continually found Daniella. She hadn't waited for him in the kitchen, hadn't looked at him when he came to the table—had only introduced him and left. Her usually sunny smile had been replaced by a stiff lift of her lips. Her bright blue eyes weren't filled with joy. They were dull. Lifeless.

A professional manner was one thing. But she seemed to be...hurt.

He analyzed their soup-and-salad conversation and couldn't find anything different about that little spat than any of their disagreements—except that he'd been smiling at her when she walked in, thinking about kissing her. Then they'd argued and he'd realized what a terrible idea kissing her was, and that had shoved even the thought of an affair out of his head.

But that was good. He should not want to get involved with an employee. No matter how pretty.

When the restaurant cleared at closing time, he left, too. He drove to his condo, showered and put on jeans and a cable-knit sweater. He hadn't been anywhere but Mancini's in weeks. Not since Christmas. And maybe that was why he was having these odd thoughts about his hostess? Maybe it was time to get out with people again? Maybe find a woman?

He shrugged into his black wool coat, took his private elevator to the building lobby and stepped outside.

His family lived in Florence, but he loved little Monte Calanetti. Rich with character and charm, the stone-and-stucco buildings on the main street housed shops run by open, friendly people. That was part of why he'd located Mancini's just outside of town. Tourists loved Monte Calanetti for its connections to the past, especially the vineyard of Palazzo di Comparino, which unfortunately had closed. But tourists still came, waiting for the day the vineyard would reopen.

Rafe's boots clicked on the cobblestone. The chill of the February night seeped into his bones. He put up the collar of his coat, trying to ward off the cold. It didn't help. When he reached Pia's Tavern, he stopped.

Inside it would be warm from a fire in the stone fireplace in the back. He could almost taste the beer from the tap. He turned and pushed open the door.

Because it was a weekday, the place was nearly empty. The television above the shelves of whiskey, gin and rum entertained the two locals sitting at the short shiny wood bar. The old squat bartender leaned against a cooler beside the four beer taps. Flames danced in the stone fireplace and warmed the small, hometown bar. As his eyes adjusted to the low lights, Rafe saw a pretty blonde girl sitting alone at a table in the back.

Dani.

He didn't know whether to shake his head or turn around and walk out. Still, when her blue eyes met his, he saw sadness that sent the heat of guilt lancing though him.

Before he could really think it through, he walked over to her table and sat across from her.

"Great. Just what every girl wants. To sit and have a drink with the boss who yells at her all day."

He frowned. "Is that why you grew so quiet today? Because I yelled at you? I didn't yell. I just didn't take your suggestion. And that is my right. I am your boss."

She sucked in a breath and reached for her beer. "Yes, I know."

"You've always known that. You ignore it, but you've always known. So this time, why are you so upset?"

She didn't reply. Instead, she reached for her coat and purse as if she intended to go. He caught her arm and stopped her.

Her gaze dropped to his hand, then met his.

Confused, he held her blue, blue eyes, as his fingers slid against her soft pink skin. The idea of having an affair with her popped into his head again. They were both incredibly passionate people and they'd probably set his bedroom on fire, if they could stop arguing long enough to kiss.

"Please. If I did something wrong, tell me—"

An unexpected memory shot through him. He hadn't cared what a woman thought since Kamila. The reminder of how he'd nearly given up his dream for her froze the rest of what he wanted to say on his tongue and forced him back to business mode.

"If you are gruff with customers I need to know why."

"I'm not gruff with customers." Her voice came out wispy and smoky.

"So it's just me, then?"

"Every time I try to be nice to you, you argue with me."

He laughed. "When did you try to be nice to me?"

"That suggestion about lunch wasn't a bad one. And I came to you politely—"

"And I listened until you wouldn't quit arguing. Then I had to stop you."

"Yes. But after that you told Emory I wasn't needed." She sniffed a laugh. "I heard you telling him you didn't even want me around."

His eyes narrowed on her face. "I tell Emory things like that all the time. I vent. It's how I get rid of stress."

"Maybe you should stop that."

He laughed, glad his feisty Dani was returning. "And maybe you should stop listening at the door?"

She shook her head and shrugged out of his hold. "I wasn't listening. You were talking loud enough that I could easily hear you through the door."

She rose to leave again. This time he had no intention of stopping her, but a wave of guilt sluiced through him. Her face was still sad. Her blue eyes dull. All because of his attempt to blow off steam.

She only got three steps before he said, "Wait! You are right. I shouldn't have said you weren't wanted. I rant to

Emory all the time. But usually no one hears me. So it doesn't matter."

She stopped but didn't return to her seat. Standing in the glow of the fireplace, she said, "If that's an apology, it's not a very good one."

No. He supposed it wasn't. But nobody ever took his rants so seriously. "Why did it upset you so much to hear you weren't wanted?"

She said nothing.

He rose and walked over to her. When she wouldn't look at him, he lifted her chin until her gaze met his. "There is a story there."

"Of course there's a story there."

He waited for her to explain, but she said nothing. The vision of her walking sadly around the restaurant filled his brain. He'd insulted hundreds of employees before, trying to get them to work harder, smarter, but from the look in her eyes he could see this was personal.

"Can you tell me?"

She shrugged away again. "So you can laugh at me?"

"I will not laugh!" He sighed, softened his voice. "Actually, I'm hoping that if you tell me it will keep me from hitting that nerve again."

"Really?"

"I'm not an idiot. I don't insult people to be cruel. When I vent to Emory it means nothing. When I yell at my employees I'm trying to get the best out of them. With you, everything's a bit different." He tossed his hands. He wouldn't tell her that part of the problem was his attraction. Especially since he went back and forth about pursuing it. Maybe if he'd just decide to take romance off the table, become her friend, things between them would get better? "It might be because you're American not European. Whatever the case, I'd like to at least know that I won't insult you again."

The bartender walked over. He gruffly threw a beer

coaster on the table, even though Dani and Rafe stood by the fireplace. "What'll it be?"

Rafe tugged Dani's hand. "Come. We'll get a nice Merlot. And talk."

She slid her hand out of his, but she did return to her seat. He named the wine he wanted from the bartender, and with a raise of his bushy brows, the bartender scrambled off to get it. When he returned with the bottle and two glasses, Rafe shooed him away, saying he'd pour.

Dani frowned. "No time for breathing?"

He chuckled. "Ah. So she thinks she knows wine?"

Her head lowered. "I don't."

His eyes narrowed as he studied her. The sad demeanor was back. The broken woman. "And all this rolls together with why I insulted you when I said you weren't wanted?"

She sighed. "Sort of. I don't know how to explain this so you'll understand, but the people I'm looking for aren't my relatives."

He smiled. "They're people who owe you money?"

She laughed. The first genuine laugh in hours and the tight ball of tension in Rafe's gut unwound.

"They are the family of the woman who was my foster mother."

"Foster mother?"

"I was taken from my mother when I was three. I don't remember her. In America, when a child has no home, he or she is placed with a family who has agreed to raise her." She sucked in a breath and took the wineglass he offered her. "Foster parents aren't required to keep you forever. So if something happens, they can give you back."

She tried to calmly give the explanation but the slight wobble of her voice when she said "give you back" caused the knot of tension to reform in Rafe's stomach. He imagined a little blue-eyed, blonde girl bouncing from home to home, hugging a scraggly brown teddy bear, and his throwaway comment about her not being wanted made his heart hurt.

"I'm sorry."

She sipped her wine. "And right about now, I'm feeling pretty stupid. You're a grouch. A perfectionist who yells at everyone. I should have realized you were venting." She met his gaze. "I'm the one who should be sorry."

"You do realize you just called me a grouch."

She took another sip of her wine. "And a perfectionist." She caught his gaze again. "See? You don't get offended."

He laughed.

She smiled.

Longing filled Rafe. For years he'd satisfied himself with one-night stands, but she made him yearn for the connection he'd had only once before. With her he wasn't Chef Rafe. She didn't treat him like a boss. She didn't talk to him like a boss...

Maybe because she had these feelings, too?

He sucked in a breath, met her gaze. "Tell me more."

"About my life?"

"About anything."

She set down her wineglass as little pinpricks of awareness sprung up on her arms.

She hadn't realized how much she'd longed for his apology until he'd made it. But now that he was asking to hear about her life, everything inside her stilled. How much to tell? How much to hold back? Why did he want to know? And why did she ache to tell him?

He offered his hand again and she glanced into his face. The lines and planes of his chin and cheeks made him classically handsome. His sexy unbound hair brought out urges in her she hadn't ever felt. She'd love to run her fingers through it while kissing him. Love to know what it would feel like to have his hair tumble to his face while they made love.

She stopped her thoughts. She had an almost fiancé at home, and Rafe wasn't the most sympathetic man in the world. He was bold and gruff, and he accepted no less than total honesty.

But maybe that's what appealed to her? She didn't want sympathy. She just wanted to talk to someone. To really be heard. To be understood.

"I had a good childhood," he said, breaking the awkward silence, again nudging his hand toward her.

She didn't take his hand, so he used it to inch her wine closer. She picked it up again.

"Even as a boy, I was fascinated by cooking."

She laughed, wondering why the hell she was tempting fate by sitting here with him when she should leave. She might not be engaged but she was close enough. And though she'd love to kiss Rafe, to run her fingers through that wild hair, Paul was stability. And she needed stability.

"My parents were initially put off, but because I also played soccer and roughhoused with my younger brother, they weren't worried."

She laughed again. He'd stopped trying to take her hand. And he really did seem to want to talk. "You make your childhood sound wonderful."

He winced. "Not intentionally."

"You don't have to worry about offending me. I don't get jealous of others' good lives. Once Rosa took me in, I had a good life."

"How old were you?"

"Sixteen."

"She was brave."

"Speaking from experience?"

"Let's just say I had a wild streak."

Looking at his hair, which curled haphazardly and made his gray eyes appear shiny and mysterious, Dani didn't doubt he had lots of women who'd helped his wild streak along.

Still, she ignored the potential to tease, to flirt, and said, "Rosa really was brave. I wasn't so much of a handful because I got into trouble, but because I was lost."

"You seem a little lost now, too."

Drat. She hadn't told him any of this for sympathy. She was just trying to keep the conversation innocent. "Seriously. You're not going to feel sorry for me, are you?"

"Not even a little bit. If you're lost now, it's your own doing. Something you need to fix yourself."

"That's exactly what I believe!"

He toasted. "To us. Two just slightly off-kilter people who make our own way."

She clinked her glass to his before taking another sip of wine. They finished their drinks in silence, which began to feel uncomfortable. If she were free, she probably would be flirting right now. But she wasn't.

Grabbing her jacket and purse, she rose from her seat. "I guess I should get going."

He rose, too. "I'll walk you to your car."

Her heart kicked against her ribs. The vision of a goodnight kiss formed in her brain. The knowledge that she'd be a cheat almost choked her. "There's no reason."

"I know. I know. It's a very peaceful little town. No reason to worry." He smiled. "Still, I've never let a woman walk to her car alone after dark."

Because that made sense, she said, "Okay." Side by side they ambled up the sidewalk to the old, battered green car Louisa had lent her.

When they reached it, she turned to him with a smile. "Thank you for listening to me. I actually feel better."

"Thank you for talking to me. Though I don't mind a little turmoil in the restaurant, I don't want real trouble."

She smiled up at him, caught the gaze of his pretty gray eyes, and felt a connection that warmed her. She didn't often tell anyone the story of her life, but he had really listened. Genuinely cared.

"So you're saying yelling is your way of creating the kind of chaos you want?"

"You make me sound like a control freak."

"You are."

He laughed. "I know."

They gazed into each other's eyes long enough for Dani's heart to begin to thrum. Knowing they were now crossing a line, she tried to pull away, but couldn't. Just when she was about to give one last shot at breaking their contact, he bent his head and kissed her.

Heat swooshed through her on a wave of surprise. Her hands slid up his arms, feeling the strength of him, and met at the back of his neck, where rich, thick hair tickled her knuckles. When he coaxed open her mouth, the taste of wine greeted her, along with a thrill so strong it spiraled through her like a tornado. The urge to press herself against him trembled through her. She'd never felt anything so powerful, so wanton. She stepped closer, enjoying sensations so intense they stole her breath.

His hands trailed from her shoulders, down her back to her bottom and that's when everything became real. What was she doing kissing someone when she had a marriage proposal waiting for her in New York?

CHAPTER FIVE

NOTHING IN RAFE'S life had prepared him for the feeling of his lips against Dani's. He told himself it was absurd for an experienced man to think one kiss different from another, but even as that thought floated to him, her lips moved, shifted, and need burst through him. She wasn't a weak woman, his Dani. She was strong, vital, and she kissed like a woman starving for the touch of a man. The kind of touch he longed to give her. And the affair was back on the table.

Suddenly, Dani jumped back, away from him. "You can't kiss me."

The wildness in her eyes mirrored the roar of need careening through him. The dew of her mouth was sprinkled on his lips. His heart pounded out an unexpected tattoo, and desire spilled through his blood.

He smiled, crossed his arms on his chest and leaned against the old car. "I think I just did."

"The point is you shouldn't kiss me."

"Because we work together?" He glanced to the right. "Bah! You Americans and your puritanical rules."

"Oh, you hate rules? What about commitments? I'm engaged!"

That stopped the need tumbling through him. That stopped the sweet swell of desire. That made him angry that she'd led him on, and feel stupid that he hadn't even suspected that a woman as pretty and cheerful as his Dani would have someone special waiting at home.

"I see."

She took three steps back, moving herself away from her own transportation. "I didn't mean to lead you on." She groaned and took another step back. "I didn't think I *was* leading you on. We were talking like friends."

He shoved off the car. "We were."

"So why'd you kiss me?"

He shrugged, as if totally unaffected, though a witch's brew of emotions careered through him like a runaway roller coaster. "It felt right." Everything about her felt right, which only annoyed him more.

She took another step away from him. "Well, it was wrong."

"If you don't stop your retreat, you're going to end up back in the tavern."

She sucked in a breath.

He opened her car door. "Get in. Go home. We're fine. I don't want you skittering around like some frightened mouse tomorrow. Let's just pretend that little kiss never happened."

He waited, holding open the door for her until he realized she wouldn't go anywhere near her car while he stood beside it. Anger punched up again. Still, keeping control, he moved away.

She sighed with relief and slid into her car.

He calmly started the walk to his condo, but when he got inside the private elevator he punched the closed door, not sure if he was angry with himself for kissing her or angry, *really angry*, that she was engaged. Taken.

He told himself not to care. Were they to have an affair, it would have been short because she was leaving, returning to America.

And even if she wasn't, even if they'd been perfect for

each other, he didn't do relationships. He knew their cost. He knew he couldn't pay it.

When the elevator doors opened again, he stepped out and tossed his keys on a convenient table in the foyer of his totally remodeled condo on the top floor of one of Monte Calanetti's most beautiful pale stone buildings. The quiet closed in on him, but he ignored it. Sometimes the price a man paid for success was his soul. He put everything he had into his meals, his restaurant, his success. He'd almost let one woman steal his dream—he wouldn't be so foolish as to even entertain the thought a second time.

The next day he worked his magic in the kitchen, confident his attraction to Dani had died with the words *I'm engaged.* He didn't stand around on pins and needles awaiting her arrival. He didn't think about her walking into the kitchen. He refused to wonder whether she'd be happy or angry. Or ponder the way he'd like to treat her to a full-course meal, watch the light in her eyes while she enjoyed the food he'd prepare especially for her...

Damn it.

What was he doing thinking about a woman who was engaged?

He walked through the dining room, checking on the tables, opening the shutters on the big windows to reveal the striking view, not at all concerned that she was late, except for how it would impact his restaurant. So when the sound of her bubbly laugher entered the dining room, and his heart stopped, he almost cursed.

Probably not seeing him in the back of the dining room, she teased with Allegra and Gio, a clear sign that the kiss hadn't affected her as much as it had affected him. He remembered the way she'd spoken to him the night before. One minute she was sad, confiding, the next she would say something like, "You should stop that." Putting him in his place. Telling him what to do. And he wondered, really, who had confided in whom the night before?

Walking to the kitchen, he ran his hand along the back of his neck. Had he really told her about his family? Not that it was any great secret, but his practice was to remain aloof. Yet, somehow, wanting to comfort her had bridged that divide and he'd talked about things he normally kept out of relationships with women.

As he approached a prep table, Emory waved a sheet of paper at him. "I've created the schedule for Daniella. I'm giving her two days off. Monday and Tuesday. Two days together, so she can sightsee."

His heart stuttered a bit, but he forced his brain to focus on work. "And just who will seat people on Monday and Tuesday?"

"Allegra has been asking for more hours. I think she'll be fine in the position as a stand-in until, as Daniella suggested, we hire two people to seat customers."

He ignored the comment about Daniella. "Allegra is willing to give up her tips?"

"She's happy with the hourly wage I suggested."

"Great. Fine. Wonderful. Maybe you should deal with staff from now on."

Emory laughed. "This was a one-time thing. A favor to Daniella. I'm a chef, too. I might play second to you, but I'm not a business manager. In fact, you're the one who's going to take this to Dani."

Ignoring the thump of his heart at having to talk to her, Rafe snatched the schedule sheet out of Emory's hands and walked out of the kitchen, into the dining room.

His gaze searched out Dani and when he found her, their eyes met. They'd shared a conversation. They'd shared a kiss. But she belonged to someone else. Any connection he felt to her stopped now.

He broke the eye contact and headed for Allegra.

"Emory tells me you're interested in earning some extra money and you're willing to be Dani's fill-in."

Her eyes brightened. *"Sì."*

"Excellent. You will come in Monday and Tuesday for Dani, then." He felt Dani's gaze burning into him, felt his face redden with color like a schoolboy in the same room with his crush. Ridiculous.

He sucked in a breath, pasted a professional smile on his face and walked over to Dani. He handed the sheet of paper to her. "You wanted a schedule. Here is your schedule."

Her blue eyes rose slowly to meet his. She said, "Thanks."

The blood in his veins slowed to a crawl. The noise in the dining room disappeared. Every nuance of their kiss flooded his memory. Along with profound disappointment that their first kiss would be their last.

He fought the urge to squeeze his eyes shut. Why was he thinking these things about a woman who was taken? All he'd wanted was an affair! Now that he knew they couldn't have one, he should just move on.

"You wanted time off. I am granting you time off."

He turned and walked away, satisfied that he sounded like his normal self. Because he was his normal self. No kiss...no *woman* would change him.

Lunch service began. Within minutes, he was caught up in the business of supervising meal prep. As course after course was served, an unexpected thought came to Rafe. An acknowledgment of something Dani had said. He didn't eat a multicourse lunch. He liked soup and salad. Was Dani right?

Dani worked her shift, struggling to ward off the tightness in her chest every time Rafe came out of the kitchen. Memories of his kiss flooded her. But the moment of pure pleasure had been darkened by the realization that she had a proposal at home...yet she'd kissed another man. And it had been a great kiss. The kind of kiss a woman loses herself in. The kind of kiss that could have swept her off her feet if she wasn't already committed.

She went home in between lunch and dinner and joined Louisa on a walk through the house as she mentally charted everything that needed to be repaired. The overwhelmed villa owner wasn't quite ready to do an actual list. It was as if Louisa needed to get her bearings or begin acclimating to the reality of the property she owned before she could do anything more than clean.

At five, Dani put on the black trousers and white blouse again and returned to the restaurant. The time went more smoothly than the lunch session, mostly because Rafe was too busy to come into the dining room, except when a customer specifically asked to speak with him. When she walked into the kitchen to get him, she kept their exchanges businesslike, and he complied, not straying into more personal chitchat. So when he asked for time with her at the end of the night again, she shivered.

She didn't think he intended to fire her. He'd just given her a schedule. He also wouldn't kiss her again. He seemed to respect the fact that there was another man in the picture, even if she had sort of stretched the truth about being *engaged*. But that was for both of their benefits. She had a proposal waiting. Her life was confusing enough already. There was no point muddying the waters with a fling. No point in leading Rafe on.

She had no idea why he wanted to talk to her, but she decided to be calm about it.

When he walked out of the kitchen, he indicated that she should sit at the bar, while he grabbed a bottle of wine.

After a sip, she smiled. "I like this one."

"So you are a fan of Chianti."

She looked at the wine in the glass, watched how the light wove through it. "I don't know if I'm a fan. But it's good." She took a quiet breath and glanced over at him. "You wanted to talk with me?"

"Today, I saw what you meant about lunch being too much food for some diners."

She turned on her seat, his reply easing her mind enough that she could be comfortable with him. "Really?"

"Yes. We should have a lunch menu. We should offer the customary meals diners expect in Italy, but we should also accommodate those who want smaller lunches."

"So I made a suggestion that you're going to use?"

He caught her gaze. "You're not a stupid woman, Dani. You know that. Otherwise, you wouldn't be so bold in your comments about the restaurant."

She grinned. "I am educated."

He shook his head. "And you have instincts." He picked up his wineglass. "I'd like you to work with me on the few selections we'll add."

Her heart sped up. "Really?"

"Yes. It was your suggestion. I believe you should have some say in the menu."

That made her laugh.

"And what is funny about that?" His voice dripped with incredulity, as if he had no idea how to follow her sometimes. His hazy gray eyes narrowed in annoyance.

She sipped her wine, delaying her answer to torment him. He was always so in control that he was cute when he was baffled. And it was fun to see him try to wrangle himself around it.

Finally she said, "You're not the big, bad wolf you want everybody to believe."

His eyes narrowed a little more as he ran his thumb along his chin. His face was perfect. Sharp angles, clean lines, accented by silvery eyes and dark, dark hair that gave him a dramatic, almost mysterious look.

"I don't mind suggestions to make the business better. Ask Emory. He's had a lot more say than you would think."

She smiled, not sure why he so desperately wanted to cling to his bossy image. "I still say you're not so bad."

* * *

Rafe's blood heated. The urge to flirt with Dani, and then seduce her, roiled like the sea before a storm. He genuinely believed she was too innocent to realize he could take her comments about his work demeanor as flirting, and shift the conversation into something personal. But he also knew they couldn't work together if she continued to be so free with him.

"Be careful what you say, little Dani, and how you take our conversations. Because I am bad. I am not the gentleman you might be accustomed to. Though I respect your engagement, if you don't, I'll take that as permission to do whatever I want. You can't have a fiancé at home and free rein to flirt here."

Her eyes widened. But he didn't give her a chance to comment. He grabbed the pad and pencil he'd brought to the bar and said, "So what should we add to this lunch menu you want?"

She licked her lips, took a slow breath as if shifting her thoughts to the task at hand and said, "Antipasto and minestrone soup. That's obvious. But you could add a garden salad, club sandwich, turkey sandwich and hamburgers." She slowly met his gaze. "That way you're serving a need without going overboard."

With the exception of the hamburger, which made him wince, he agreed. "I can put my own spin on all of these, use the ingredients we already have on hand, redo the menu tonight and we'll be ready to go tomorrow."

She gaped at him. "Tomorrow? Wow."

He rose. "This is my business, Dani. If a suggestion is good, there is no point waiting forever. I get things done. Go home. I will see you tomorrow."

She walked to the door, and he headed for the kitchen where he could watch her leave from the window above the sink, making sure nothing happened to her. No matter how hard he tried to stop it, disappointment rose up in him. At the very least, it would have been nice to finish a glass of wine with her.

But he couldn't.

Dani ran to her car, her blood simmering, her nerve endings taut. They might have had a normal conversation about his menu. She might have even left him believing she was okay with everything he'd said and they were back to normal. But she couldn't forget his declaration that he was bad. It should have scared her silly. Instead, it tempted her. She'd never been attracted to a man who was clearly all wrong for her, a man with whom she couldn't have a future. Everything she did was geared toward security. Everything about him spelled danger.

So why was he so tempting?

Walking into the kitchen of Louisa's run-down villa, she found her friend sitting at the table with a cup of tea.

Louisa smiled as she entered. "Can I get you a cup?"

She squeezed her eyes shut. "I don't know."

Louisa rose. "What's wrong? You're shaking."

She dropped to one of the chairs at the round table. "Rafe and I had a little chat after everyone was gone."

"Did he fire you?"

"I think I might have welcomed that."

Louisa laughed. "You need a cup of tea." She walked to the cupboard, retrieved the tin she'd bought in the village, along with enough groceries for the two of them, and ran water into the kettle. "So what did he say?"

"He told me to be careful where I took our conversations."

"Are you insulting him again?"

"He danced around it a bit, but he thinks I'm flirting with him."

Eyes wide, Louisa turned from the stove. "Are you?"

Dani pressed her lips together before she met Louisa's gaze. "Not intentionally. You know I have a fiancé."

"Sounds like you're going to have to change the way you act around Rafe, then. Treat him the way he wants to be treated, like a boss you respect. Mingle with the waitstaff. Enjoy your job. But stay away from him."

The next day, Rafe stacked twenty-five black leather folders containing the new menus on the podium for Dani to distribute when she seated customers.

An hour later, she entered the kitchen, carrying them. Her smile as radiant as the noonday sun, she said, "These look great."

Rafe nodded, moving away from her, reminding himself that she was engaged to another man. "As I told you last night, this is a business. Good ideas are always welcome."

Emory peeked around Rafe. "And, please, if you have any more ideas, don't hesitate to offer them."

Rafe said, "Bah," and walked away. But he saw his old, bald friend wink at Dani as if they were two conspirators. At first, he was comforted that Emory had also succumbed to Dani's charms, but he knew that was incorrect. Emory liked Dani as a person. While Rafe wanted to sleep with her. But as long as he reminded himself his desires were wrong, he could control them.

Customer response to the lunch menu was astounding. Dani took no credit for the new offerings and referred comments and compliments to him. Still, she was in the spotlight everywhere he went. Customers loved her. The waitstaff deferred to her. Her smile lit the dining room. Her laughter floated on the air. And he was glad when she said goodbye at the end of the day, if only so he could get some peace.

Monday morning, he arrived at the restaurant and breathed in the scent of the business he called home. Today would be a good day because Dani was off. For two glorious days he would not have to watch his words, watch where his eyes went or control hormones he didn't understand. Plus, her having two days off was a great way to transition his thoughts away from her as a person and to her as an employee.

And who knew? Maybe Allegra would work so well as a hostess that he could actually cut Dani's hours even more. Not in self-preservation over his unwanted attraction, but because this was a business. He was the boss. And the atmosphere of the restaurant would go back to normal.

As Emory supervised the kitchen, Rafe interviewed two older gentlemen for Dani's job. Neither was suitable, but he comforted himself with the knowledge that this was only his first attempt at finding her replacement. He had other interviews scheduled for that afternoon and the next day. He *would* replace her.

Allegra arrived on time to open for lunch. Because they were enjoying an unexpected warm spell, he opened the windows and let the breeze spill in. The scents of rich Tuscan foods drifted from the kitchen. And just as Rafe expected, suddenly, all became right with the world.

Until an hour later when he heard a clang and a clatter from the dining room. He set down his knife and stormed out. Gio had dropped a tray of food when Allegra had knocked into her.

"What is this?" he asked, his hands raised in confusion. "You navigate around each other every day. Now, today, you didn't see her?"

Allegra stooped to help Gio pick up the broken dishes. "I'm sorry. It's just nerves. I was turned away, talking to the customer and didn't watch where I was going."

"Bah! Nerves. Get your head on straight!"

Allegra nodded quickly and Rafe returned to the kitchen. He summoned the two busboys to the dining room to clean up the mess and everything went back to normal.

Except customers didn't take to Allegra. She was sweet, but she wasn't fun. She wasn't chatty. A lifelong resident, she didn't see Italy through the eyes of someone who loved it with the passion and intensity of a newcomer as Dani did.

One customer even asked for her. Rafe smiled and said she had a day off. The customer asked for the next shift she'd be working so he could return and tell her of his trip to Venice.

"She'll be back on Wednesday," Rafe said. He tried to pretend he didn't feel the little rise in his heart at the thought of her return, but he'd felt it. After only a few hours, he missed her.

CHAPTER SIX

AND SHE MISSED HIM.

The scribbled notes of things she remembered her foster mother telling her about her Italian relatives hadn't helped her to find them. But Dani discovered stepping stones to people who knew people who knew people who would ultimately get her to the ones she wanted.

Several times she found herself wondering how Rafe would handle the situation. Would he ask for help? What would he say? And she realized she missed him. She didn't mind his barking. He'd shown her a kinder side. She remembered the conversation in which he'd told her about his family. She loved that he'd taken her suggestion about a lunch menu. But most of all, she replayed that kiss over and over and over in her head, worried because she couldn't even remember her first kiss with Paul.

Steady, stable Paul hadn't ever kissed her like Rafe had. Ever. But he had qualities Rafe didn't have. Stability being number one. He was an accountant at a bank, for God's sake. A man did not get any more stable than that. She'd already had a life of confusion and adventure of a sort, when she was plucked from one foster home and dropped in another. She didn't want confusion or danger or adventure. She wanted stability.

That night when she called Paul, he immediately asked

when she was returning. Her heart lifted a bit hearing that. "I hate talking on the phone."

It was the most romantic thing he'd ever said to her. Until he added, "I'd rather just wait until you get home to talk."

"Oh."

"Now, don't get pouty. You know you have a tendency to talk too much."

She *was* chatty.

"Anyway, I'm at work. I've got to go."

"Oh. Okay."

"Call me from your apartment when you get home."

She frowned. Home? Did he not want to talk to her for an entire month? "Aren't you going to pick me up at the airport?"

"Maybe, but you'll probably be getting in at rush hour or something. Taking a taxi would be easier, wouldn't it? We'll see how the time works out."

"I guess that makes sense."

"Good. Gotta run."

Even as she disconnected the call, she thought of Rafe. She couldn't see him telling his almost fiancée to call when she arrived at her apartment after nearly seven months without seeing each other. He'd race to the airport, grab her in baggage claim and kiss her senseless.

Her breath vanished when she pictured the scene, and she squeezed her eyes shut. She really could not think like that. She absolutely couldn't start comparing Paul and Rafe. Especially not when it came to passion. Poor sensible Paul would always suffer by comparison.

Plus, her feelings for Rafe were connected to the rush of pleasure she got from finding a place in his restaurant, being more than useful, offering ideas a renowned chef had implemented. For a former foster child, having somebody give her a sense of worth and value was like gold.

And that's all it was. Attraction to his good looks and

appreciation that he recognized and told her she was doing a good job.

She did not want him.

Really.

She needed somebody like Paul.

Though she knew that was true, it didn't sit right. She couldn't stop thinking about the way he didn't want to pick her up at the airport, how he'd barely had two minutes to talk to her and how he'd told her not to call again.

She tried to read, tried to chat with Louisa about the house, but in the end, she knew she needed to get herself out of the house or she'd make herself crazy.

She told Louisa she was going for a drive and headed into town.

Antsy, unable to focus, and afraid he was going to royally screw something up and disappoint a customer, Rafe turned Mancini's over to Emory.

"It's not like you to leave so early."

"It's already eight o'clock." Rafe shrugged into his black wool coat. "Maybe too many back-to-back days have made me tired."

Emory smiled. "Ah, so maybe like Dani, you need a day off?"

Buttoning his coat, he ignored the dig and walked to the back door. "I'll see you tomorrow."

But as he was driving through town, he saw the ugly green car Dani drove sitting at the tavern again. The last time she'd been there had been the day he'd inadvertently insulted her. She didn't seem like the type to frequent taverns, so what if she was upset again?

His heart gave a kick and he whipped his SUV into a parking place, raced across the quiet street and entered the tavern to find her at the same table she'd been at before.

He walked over. She glanced up.

Hungrier for the sight of her than was wise, he held her

gaze as he slid onto the chair across from her. "So this is how you spend your precious time off."

She shook her head. "Don't start."

He hadn't meant to be argumentative. In fact that was part of their problem. There was no middle with them. They either argued or lusted after each other. Given that he was her boss and she was engaged, both were wrong.

The bartender ambled over. He set a coaster in front of Rafe with a sigh. "You want another bottle of that fancy wine?"

Rafe shook his head and named one of the beers on tap before he pointed to Dani's glass. "And another of whatever she's having."

As the bartender walked away, she said, "You don't have to buy me a beer."

"I'm being friendly because I think we need to find some kind of balance." He was tired of arguing, but he also couldn't go on thinking about her all the time. The best way to handle both would be to classify their relationship as a friendship. Tonight, he could get some questions answered, get to know her and see that she was just like everybody else. Not somebody special. Then they could both go back to normal.

"Balance?"

He shrugged. Leaning back, he anchored his arm across the empty chair beside him. "We're either confiding like people who want to become lovers, or we fight."

She turned her beer glass nervously. "That's true."

"So, we drink a beer together. We talk about inconsequential things, and Wednesday when you return to Mancini's, no one snipes."

She laughed.

He smiled. "What did you do today?"

"I went to the town where my foster mother's relatives lived."

His beer arrived. Waiting for her to elaborate, he took

a sip. Then another. When she didn't say anything else, he asked, "So did you find them?"

"Not yet. But I will."

Her smooth skin virtually glowed. Her blue eyes met his. Interest and longing swam through him. He ignored both in favor of what now seemed to be a good mission. Becoming friends. Finding a middle ground where they weren't fighting or lusting, but a place where they could coexist.

"What did you do today?"

"Today I created a lasagna that should have made customers die from pleasure."

She laughed. "Exaggerate much?"

He pointed a finger at her. "It's not an exaggeration. It's confidence."

"Ah."

"You don't like confidence?"

She studied his face. "Maybe it's more that I don't trust it."

"What's to trust? I love to cook, to make people happy, to surprise them with something wonderful. But I didn't just open a door to my kitchen and say, come eat this. I went to school. I did apprenticeships. My confidence is in my teachers' ability to take me to the next level as much as it is in my ability to learn, and then do."

Her head tilted. "So it's not all about you."

He laughed, shook his head. "Where do you get these ideas?"

"You're kind of arrogant."

He batted his hand. "Arrogant? Confident? Who cares as long as the end result is good?"

"I guess…"

"I know." He took another sip of beer, watching as she slid her first drink—which he assumed was warm—aside and reached for the second glass he'd bought for her. "Not much of a drinker?"

"No."

"So what are you?"

She laughed. "Is this how you become friends with someone?"

"Conversation is how everyone becomes friends."

"I thought it was shared experience."

"We don't have time for shared experience. If we want to become friends by Wednesday we need to take shortcuts."

She inclined her head as if agreeing.

He waited. When she said nothing, he reframed his question. "So you are happy teaching?"

"I'm a good teacher."

"But you are not happy?"

"I'm just not sure people are supposed to be happy."

He blinked. That was the very last thing he'd expected to hear from his bubbly hostess. "Seriously?"

She met his gaze. "Yeah. I think we're meant to be content. I think we're meant to find a spot and fill it. But happy? That's reserved for big events or holidays."

For thirty seconds, he wished she were staying in Italy. He wished he had time enough to show her the sights, teach her the basics of cooking, make her laugh, show her what happiness was. But that wasn't the mission. The mission was to get to know her just enough that they would stop arguing.

"This from my happy, upbeat hostess?"

She met his gaze again. "I thought we weren't going to talk about work."

"We're talking about you, not work."

She picked up her beer glass. "Maybe this isn't the best time to talk about me."

Which only filled him with a thousand questions. When she was at Mancini's she was usually joyful. After a day off, she was as sad as the day he'd hurt her feelings? It made no sense...unless he believed that she loved working in his restaurant enough that it filled her with joy.

That made his pulse jump, made his mind race with thoughts he wasn't supposed to have. So he rose.

"Okay. Talking is done. We'll try shared experience." He pointed behind her. "We'll play darts."

Clearly glad they'd no longer be talking, she laughed. "Good."

"So you play darts at home in New York?"

She rose and followed him to the board hung on a back wall. They passed the quiet pool table, and he pulled some darts from the corkboard beside the dartboard.

"No, I don't play darts."

"Great. So we play for money?"

She laughed again. "No! We'll play for fun."

He sighed as if put out. "Too bad."

But as they played, she began to talk about her search for her foster mother's family. Her voice relaxed. Her smile returned. And Rafe was suddenly glad he'd found her. Not for his mission to make her his friend. But because she was alone. And in spite of her contention that people weren't supposed to be happy, her normal state was happy. He'd seen that every day at the restaurant. But something had made her sad tonight.

Reminded of the way he had made her sad by saying she wasn't needed, he redoubled his efforts to make her smile.

It was easy for Dani to dismiss the significance of Rafe finding her in the bar. They lived in a small town. He didn't have a whole hell of a lot of choices for places to stop after work. So she wouldn't let her crazy brain tell her it was sweet that he'd found her. She'd call it what it was. Lack of options.

Playing darts with her, Rafe was kind and polite, but not sexy. At least not deliberately sexy. There were some things a really handsome man couldn't control. So she didn't think he was coming on to her when he swaggered over to pull the darts from the board after he threw them. She didn't think he was trying to entice her when he laughed at her poor attempts at hitting the board. And she absolutely made nothing of it when he stood behind her, took her arm and showed her the motion she needed to make to get the dart going in the right direction.

Even though she could smell him, feel the heat of his body as he brushed up against her back, and feel the vibrations of his warm whisper as he pulled her arm back and demonstrated how to aim, she knew he meant nothing by any of it. He just wanted to be friends.

When their third beer was gone and the hour had gotten late, she smiled at him. "Thank you. That was fun."

His silver eyes became serious. "You were happy?"

She shook her head at his dog-with-a-bone attitude. "Sort of. Yes. It was a happy experience."

He sniffed and walked back to their table to retrieve his coat. "Everyone is made to be happy."

She didn't believe that. Though she liked her life and genuinely liked people, she didn't believe her days were supposed to be one long party. But she knew it was best not to argue. She joined him at their table and slipped into her coat.

"I'll walk you to your car."

She shook her head. "No." Their gazes caught. "I'm fine."

He dipped his head in a quick nod, agreeing, and she walked out into the cold night. Back into the world where her stable fiancé wouldn't even pick her up at the airport.

CHAPTER SEVEN

WHEN DANI ENTERED the restaurant on Wednesday ten minutes before the start of her shift, Rafe stood by the bar, near the kitchen. As if he'd sensed her arrival, he turned. Their gazes caught. Dani's heart about pounded its way out of her chest. She reminded herself that though they'd spent an enjoyable evening together playing darts at the tavern, for him it had been about becoming friends. He hadn't made any passes at her—though he'd had plenty of chances—and he'd made a very good argument for why being friends was a wise move for them.

Still, when he walked toward her, her heart leaped. But he passed the podium to unlock the front door. As he turned to return to the kitchen, he said, "Good morning."

She cleared her throat, hoping to rid it of the fluttery feeling floating through her at being in the same room with him. Especially since they were supposed to be friends now. Nothing more. "Good morning."

"How did your search go for your foster mother's relatives yesterday?"

She shook her head. "Still haven't found them, but I got lots of information from people who had been their neighbors. Most believe they moved to Rome."

"Rome?" He shook his head. "No kidding."

"Their former neighbors said something about one of

their kids getting a job there and the whole family wanting to stay together."

"Nice. Family should stay together."

"I agree."

She turned to the podium. He walked to the kitchen.
But she couldn't help thinking that while Paul hadn't said
a word about her quest for Rosa's family, Rafe had immediately asked. Like someone who cared about her versus
someone who didn't.

She squeezed her eyes shut and told herself not to think
like that. They were *friends. Only friends.*

But all day, she was acutely aware of him. Anytime
she retrieved him to escort him to a table, she felt him all
around her. Her skin tingled. Everything inside her turned
soft and feminine.

At the end of the night, the waitstaff and kitchen help
disappeared like rats on a sinking ship. Rafe ambled to the
bar, pulled a bottle of wine from the rack behind it.

The Chianti. The wine he'd ordered for them at the tavern.

Her heart trembled. She'd told him she liked that wine.

Was he asking her to stay now? To share another bottle
of the wine she'd said she liked?

Longing filled her and she paused by the podium. When
he didn't even look in her direction, she shuffled a bit, hoping the movement would cause him to see her and invite
her to stay.

He kept his gaze on a piece of paper sitting on the bar
in front of him. Still, she noticed a second glass by the
bottle. He had poured wine in one glass but the other was
empty—yet available.

She bit her lip. Was that glass an accident? An oversight?
Or was that glass her invitation?

She didn't know. And things were going so well between

them professionally that she didn't want to make a mistake that took them back to an uncomfortable place.

Still, they'd decided to be friends. Wouldn't a friend want another friend to share a glass of wine at the end of the night?

She drew in a slow breath. She had one final way to get him to notice her and potentially invite her to sit with him. If he didn't take this hint, then she would leave.

Slowly, cautiously, she called, "Good night."

He looked over. He hesitated a second, but only a second, before he said, "Good night."

Disappointment stopped her breathing. Nonetheless, she smiled and headed for the door. She walked to Louisa's beat-up old car, got in, slid the key in the ignition...

And lowered her head to the steering wheel.

She wanted to talk to him. She wanted to tell him about the countryside she'd seen as she looked for Rosa's relatives. She longed to tell him about the meals she'd eaten. She yearned to ask him how the restaurant had been the two days she was gone. She needed to get not just the cursory answers he'd given her but the real in-depth stuff. Like a friend.

But she also couldn't lie to herself. She wanted that crazy feeling he inspired in her. Lust or love, hormones or genuine attraction, she had missed that feeling. She'd missed *him*. No matter how much she told herself she just wanted to be his friend, it was a lie.

A light tapping on her window had her head snapping up.

Rafe.

She quickly lowered the window to see what he wanted. "Are you okay?"

Her heart swelled, then shrank and swelled again. Everything he did confused her. Everything she felt around him confused her even more.

"Are you ill?"

She shook her head.

Damn it. She squeezed her eyes shut and decided to just go with the truth. "I saw you with the wine and thought I should have joined you." She caught the gaze of his smoky-gray eyes. "You said we were going to be friends. And I was hoping you sitting at the bar with a bottle of wine was an invitation."

He stepped back. She'd never particularly thought of a chef's uniform as being sexy, but he'd taken off the jacket, revealing a white T-shirt that outlined muscles and a flat stomach. Undoubtedly hot from working in the kitchen, he didn't seem bothered by the cold night air.

"I always have a glass of wine at the end of the night."

So, her instincts had been wrong. If she'd just started her car and driven off, she wouldn't be embarrassed right now. "Okay. Good."

He glanced down into the car at her. "But I wouldn't have minded company."

Embarrassment began to slide away, only to be replaced by the damnable confusion. "Oh."

"I simply don't steal women who belong to other men."

"It wouldn't be stealing if we were talking about work, becoming friends like you said we should."

"That night was a one-time thing. A way to get to know each other so we could stop aggravating each other."

"So we're really not friends?"

He laughed and glanced away at the beautiful starlit sky. "We're now friendly enough to work together. Men only try to become 'real' friends so that they can ultimately become lovers."

The way he said *lovers* sent a wave of yearning skittering along her nerve endings. It suddenly became difficult to breathe.

He caught her gaze again. "I've warned you before to be careful with me, Dani. I'm not a man who often walks away from what he wants."

"Wow. You are one honest guy."

He laughed. "Usually I wouldn't care. I'd muscle my way into your life and take what I wanted. But you're different. You're innocent."

"I sort of liked being different until you added the part about me being innocent."

"You are."

"Well, yeah. Sort of." She tossed her hands in exasperation, the confusion and longing getting the better of her. "But you make it sound like a disease."

"It's not. It's actually a quality men look for in a woman they want to keep."

Her heart fluttered again. "Oh?"

"Don't get excited about that. I'm not the kind of guy who commits. I like short-term relationships because I don't like complications. I'm attracted to you, yes, but I also know myself. My commitment to the restaurant comes before any woman." He forced her gaze to his again. "This thing I feel for you is wrong. So as much as I wanted you to take the hint tonight and share a bottle of wine with me, I also hoped you wouldn't. I don't want to hurt you."

"We could always talk about the restaurant."

"About how you were missed? How a customer actually asked for you?"

She laughed. "See? That's all great stuff. Neutral stuff."

"I suppose you also wouldn't be opposed to hearing that Emory thinks that after the success of your lunch menu, we should encourage you to make suggestions."

Pride flooded her. "Well, I'll do my best to think of new things."

He glanced at the stars again. Their conversation had run its course. He stood in the cold. She sat in a car that could be warm if she'd started the darn thing. But the air between them was anything but cool, and she suddenly realized they were kidding themselves if they believed they could be just friends.

He looked down and smiled slightly. "Good night, Dani."

He didn't wait for her to say good-night. He walked away.

She sat there for a few seconds, tingling, sort of breathless, but knowing he was right. They couldn't be friends and they couldn't have a fling. She *was* innocent and he would hurt her. And though technically she'd stretched the truth about being engaged, it was saving her heartbreak.

After starting her car, she pulled out, watching in the rearview mirror as he revved the engine of his big SUV and followed her to Monte Calanetti.

Though Dani dressed in her usual black trousers and white blouse the next morning, she took extra care when she ironed them, making them crisper, their creases sharper, so she looked more professional when she arrived at the restaurant.

Rafe spoke sparingly. It wasn't long before she realized that unless she had a new idea to discuss, they wouldn't interact beyond his thank-you when she introduced him to a customer who wanted to compliment the chef.

She understood. Running into each other at the tavern the first time and talking out their disagreement, then playing darts the second, had made them friendly enough that they no longer sniped. But having minimal contact with her was how he would ignore their attraction. They weren't right for each other and, older, wiser, he was sparing them both. But that didn't really stop her attraction to him.

To keep herself from thinking about Rafe on Friday, she studied the customer seating, the china and silverware, the interactions of the waitresses with the customers, but didn't come up with an improvement good enough to suggest to him.

A thrill ran through her at the knowledge that he took her ideas so seriously. Here she was, an educated but simple girl from Brooklyn, being taken seriously by a lauded European chef.

The sense of destiny filled her again, along with Rafe's comment about happiness. This time her thoughts made her gasp. What if this feeling of rightness wasn't about Rafe or Italy? What if this sense of being where she belonged was actually telling her the truth about her career choice? She loved teaching, but it didn't make her feel she belonged the way being a part of this restaurant did. And maybe this sense of destiny was simply trying to point her in the direction of a new career when she returned to the United States?

The thought relieved her. Life was so much simpler when the sense of destiny was something normal, like an instinct for the restaurant business, rather than longing for her boss—a guy she shouldn't even be flirting with when she had a marriage proposal waiting for her at home.

Emory came to the podium and interrupted her thoughts. "These are the employee phone numbers. Gio called off sick for tonight's shift. I'd like you to call in a replacement."

She glanced up at him. "Who should I call?"

He smiled. "Your choice. Being out here all the time, you know who works better with whom."

After calling Zola, she walked back to the kitchen to return the list.

Emory shook his head. "This is your responsibility now. A new job for you, while you're here, to make my life a little easier."

She smiled. "Okay."

Without looking at her, Rafe said, "We'd also like you to begin assigning tasks to the busboys. After you say goodbye to a guest, we'd like you to come in and get the busboys. That will free up the waitresses a bit."

The feeling of destiny swelled in her again. The new tasks felt like a promotion, and there wasn't a person in the world who didn't like being promoted.

When Rafe refused to look at her, she winked at Emory. "Okay."

Walking back to the dining room, she fought the feeling that her destiny, her gift, was for this particular restaurant. Especially since, when returning to New York, she'd start at the bottom of any dining establishment she chose to work, and that would be a problem since she'd only make minimum wage. At Mancini's, she only needed to earn extra cash. In New York, would a job as a hostess support her?

The next day, Lazare, one of the busboys, called her "Miss Daniella." The shift from Dani to Miss Daniella caught on in the kitchen and the show of respect had Daniella's shoulders straightening with confidence. When she brought Rafe out for a compliment from a customer, even he said, "Thank you, Miss Daniella," and her heart about popped out of her chest with pride.

That brought her back to the suspicion that her sense of destiny wasn't for the restaurant business, but for *this* restaurant and these people. If she actually got a job at a restaurant in New York, she couldn't expect the staff there to treat her this well.

Realizing all her good fortune would stop when she left Mancini's, her feeling of the "destiny" of belonging in the restaurant business fizzled. She would go home to a tiny apartment, a man whose marriage proposal had scared her and a teaching position that suddenly felt boring.

"Miss Daniella," Gio said as she approached the podium later that night. "The gentleman at table two would like to speak to the chef."

She said it calmly, but there was an undercurrent in her voice, as if subtly telling Daniella that this was a problem situation, not a compliment.

She smiled and said, "Thank you, Gio. I'll handle it."

She walked over to the table.

The short, stout man didn't wait for Dani to speak. He immediately said, "My manicotti was dry and tasteless."

Daniella inclined her head in acknowledgment of his comment. "I'm sorry. I'm not sure what happened. I'll tell the kitchen staff."

"I want to talk to the chef."

His loud, obnoxious voice carried to the tables around him. Daniella peeked behind her at the kitchen door, then glanced at the man again. The restaurant had finally freed itself of people curious about Rafe's temper. The seats had filled with customers eager to taste his food. She would not let his reputation be ruined by a beady-eyed little man who probably wanted a free dinner.

"We're extremely busy tonight," she told the gentleman as she looped her fingers around his biceps and gently urged him to stand. "So rather than a chat with the chef, what if I comp your dinner?"

His eyes widened, then returned to normal, as if he couldn't believe he was getting what he wanted so easily. "You'll pay my tab?"

She smiled. "The whole meal." A quick glance at the table told her that would probably be the entire day's wage, but it would be worth it to avoid a scene.

"I'd like dessert."

"We'll get it for you to go." She nodded to Gio, who quickly put two slices of cake into a take-out container and within seconds the man and his companion were gone.

Rafe watched from the sliver of a crack he created when he pushed open the kitchen door a notch. He couldn't hear what Dani said, but he could see her calm demeanor, her smiles, the gentle but effective way she removed the customer from Rafe's dining room without the other patrons being any the wiser.

He laughed and Emory walked over.

"What's funny?"

"Dani just kicked somebody out."

Emory's eyes widened. "We had a scene?"

"That's the beauty of it. Even though he started off yelling, she got him out without causing even a ripple of trouble. I'll bet the people at the adjoining tables weren't even aware of what was happening beyond his initial grousing."

"She is worth her weight in gold."

Rafe pondered that. "Gio made the choice to get her rather than come to me."

Emory said, "She trusts Dani."

He walked away, leaving Rafe with that simple but loaded thought.

At the end of the night, the waitstaff quickly finished their cleanup and began leaving before the kitchen staff. Rafe glanced at the bar, thought about a glass of wine and decided against it. Instead, he walked to the podium as Dani collected her purse.

He waited for the waitresses on duty to leave before he faced Dani.

"You did very well tonight."

"Thank you."

"I saw you get rid of the irate customer."

She winced. "I had to offer to pay for his meal."

"I'll take care of that."

Her gaze met his, tripping the weird feeling in his chest again.

"Really?"

"Yes." He sucked in a breath, reminding himself he didn't want the emotions she inspired in him. He wanted a good hostess. He didn't want a fling with another man's woman.

"I trust your judgment. If not charging for his food avoided a scene, I'm happy to absorb the cost."

"Thanks."

He glanced away, then looked back at her. "Your duties just keep growing."

"Is this your subtle way of telling me I overstepped?"

He shook his head. "You take work that Emory and I would have to do. Things we truly do not have time for."

"Which is good?"

"Yes. Very good." He gazed into her pretty blue eyes and fought the desire to kiss her that crept up before he could stop it. His restaurant was becoming exactly what he'd envisioned because of her. Because she knew how to direct diners' attention and mood. It was as if they were partners in his venture and though the businessman in him desperately fought his feelings for her, the passionate part of him wanted to lift her off the ground, swing her around and kiss her ardently.

But that was wrong for so many reasons that he got angry with himself for even considering it.

"I was thinking tonight that a differentiation between you and the waitresses would be good. It would be a show of authority."

"You want me to wear a hat?"

He laughed. Was it any wonder he was so drawn to her? No one could so easily catch him off guard. Make him laugh. Make him wish for a life that included a little more fun.

"I want you to wear something other than the dark trousers and white blouses the waitresses wear. Your choice," he said when her face turned down with a puzzled frown. "A dress. A suit. Anything that makes you look like you're in charge."

Her gaze rose to meet his. "In charge?"

"Of the dining room." He laughed lightly. "You still have a few weeks before I give you my job."

She laughed, too.

But when her laughter died, they were left gazing into each other's eyes. The mood shifted from happy and businesslike to something he couldn't define or describe. The click of connection he always felt with her filled him. It was hot and sweet, but pointless, leaving an emptiness in the pit of his stomach.

He said, "Good night, Dani," and walked away, into the kitchen and directly to the window over the sink. A minute later, he watched her amble across the parking lot to her car, start it and drive off, making sure she had no trouble.

Then he locked the restaurant and headed to his SUV.

He might forever remember the joy in her blue eyes when he told her that he wanted her to look like the person of authority in the dining room.

But as he climbed into his vehicle, his smile faded. Here he was making her happy, giving her promotions, authority, and just when he should have been able to kiss her to celebrate, he'd had to pull back...because she was taken.

Was he crazy to keep her on, to continually promote her, to need her for his business when it was clear that there was no chance of a relationship between them?

Was he being a sucker?

Was she using him?

Bah! What the hell was he doing? Thinking about things that didn't matter? The woman was leaving in a few weeks. And that was the real reason he should worry about depending on her. Soon she would be gone. So why were he and Emory leaning on her?

Glad he had more maître d' interviews scheduled for the following Monday, he started his car and roared out of the parking lot. He would use what he had learned about Dani's duties for his new maître d'. But he wouldn't give her any more authority.

And he absolutely would stop all thoughts about wanting to swing her around, kiss her and enjoy their success. It was not "their" success. It was his.

It was also her choice to have no part in it.

Sunday morning, Dani arrived at the restaurant in a slim cream-colored dress. She had curled her hair and pinned it in a bundle on top of her head. When Rafe saw her his jaw fell.

She looked regal, sophisticated. Perfect as the face of his business.

Emory whistled. "My goodness."

Rafe's breath stuttered into his lungs. He reminded himself of his thoughts from the night before. She was leaving. She wanted no part in his long-term success. He and Emory were depending on her too much for someone who had no plans to stay.

But most of all, leaving was her choice.

She didn't want him or his business in her life. She was here only for some money so she could find the relatives of her foster mother.

The waitresses tittered over how great she looked. Emory walked to the podium, took her hands and kissed both of her cheeks. The busboys blushed every time she was near.

She handled it with a cool grace that spoke of dignity and sophistication. Exactly what he wanted as the face of Mancini's. As if she'd read his mind.

Laughing with Allegra, she said, "I feel like I'm playing dress up. These are Louisa's clothes. I don't own anything so pretty."

Allegra sighed with appreciation. "Well, they're perfect for you and your new position."

She laughed again. "Rafe and Emory only promoted me because I have time on my hands in between customers. While you guys are hustling, I'm sort of looking around, figuring things out." She leaned in closer. "Besides, the extra authority doesn't come with more money."

As Allegra laughed, Rafe realized that was true. Unless Dani was a power junkie, she wasn't getting anything out of her new position except more work.

So why did she look so joyful in a position she'd be leaving in a few weeks?

Sunday lunch was busier than normal. Customers came in, ate, chatted with Dani and left happy.

Which relieved Rafe and also caused him to internally scold himself for distrusting her. He didn't know why she'd taken such an interest in his restaurant, but he should be glad she had.

She didn't leave for the space between the last lunch customer and the first dinner customer because the phone never stopped ringing.

Again, Rafe relaxed a bit. She had good instincts. Now that his restaurant was catching on, there were more dinner reservations. She stayed to take them. She was a good, smart employee. Any mistrust he had toward her had to be residual bad feelings over not being able to pursue her when he so desperately wanted to. His fault. Not hers.

In fact, part of him believed he should apologize. Or maybe not apologize. Since she couldn't see inside his brain and know the crazy thoughts he'd been thinking, a compliment would work better.

He walked out of the kitchen to the podium and smiled when he saw she was on the phone. Their reservations for that night would probably be their best ever.

"So we're talking about a hundred people."

Rafe's eyebrows rose. A hundred people? He certainly hoped that wasn't a single reservation for that night. Yes, there was a private room in which he could probably seat a hundred, but because that room was rarely used, those tables and chairs needed to be wiped down. Extra linens would have to be ordered from their vendor. Not to mention enough food. He needed advance warning to serve a hundred people over their normal customer rate.

He calmed himself. She didn't know that the room hadn't been used in months and would need a good dusting. Or about the linens. Or the extra food. Once he told her, they could discuss the limits on reservations.

When she finally replaced the receiver on the phone, her blue eyes glowed.

Need rose inside him. Once again he fought the unwanted urge to share the joy of success with her. No matter how he sliced it, she was a big part of building his clientele. And rather than worry about her leaving, a smart businessman would be working to entice her to stay. To make *his* business *her* career, and Italy her new home.

Romantic notions quickly replaced his business concerns. If she made Italy her home, she might just leave her fiancé in America, and he could—

Realizing he wasn't just getting ahead of himself, he was going in the wrong direction, he forced himself to be professional. "It sounds like you got us a huge reservation."

"Better."

He frowned. "Better? How does something get better than a hundred guests for dinner?"

She grinned. "By catering a wedding! They don't even need our dishes and utensils. The venue is providing that. All they want is food. And for you that's easy."

Rafe blinked. "What?"

"Okay, it's like this. A customer came in yesterday. The dinner they chose was what his wife wanted to be served for their daughter's wedding at the end of the month. When they ate your meal, they knew they wanted you to cook food for their daughter's wedding. The bride's dad called, I took down the info," she said, handing him a little slip. "And now we have a new arm of your business."

Anything romantic he felt for Dani shrank back against the rising tide of red-hot anger.

"I am not a caterer."

He controlled his voice, didn't yell, didn't pounce. But he saw recognition come to Dani's eyes. She might have only worked with him almost two weeks, but she knew him.

Her fingers fluttered to her throat. "I thought you'd be pleased."

"I have a business plan. I have Michelin stars to protect. I will not send my food out into the world for God knows who to do God knows what with it."

She swallowed. "You could go to the wedding—"

"And leave the restaurant?"

She sucked in a breath.

"Call them back and tell them you checked with me and we can't deliver."

"But...I..." She swallowed again. "They needed a commitment. Today. I gave our word."

He gaped at her. "You promised something without asking me?" It was the cardinal sin. The unforgivable sin. Promising something that hadn't been approved because she'd never consulted the boss. Every employee knew that. She hadn't merely overstepped. She'd gone that one step too far.

Her voice was a mere whisper when she said, "Yes."

Anger mixed with incredulity at her presumptuousness, and he didn't hesitate. With his dream in danger, he didn't even have to think about it. "You're fired."

CHAPTER EIGHT

"Leave now."

Dani's breaths came in quick, shallow puffs. No one wanted to be fired. But right at that moment she wasn't concerned about her loss. Her real upset came from failing Rafe. She'd thought he'd be happy with the added exposure. Instead, she'd totally misinterpreted the situation. Contrary to her success in the dining room, she wasn't a chef. She didn't know a chef's concerns. She had no real restaurant experience.

Still, she had instincts—

Didn't she?

"I'll fix this."

He turned away. "This isn't about fixing the problem. This is about you truly overstepping this time. I don't know if it's because we've had personal conversations or because to this point all of your ideas have been good. But no one, absolutely no one, makes such an important decision without my input. You are fired."

He walked into the kitchen without looking back. Dani could have followed him, maybe even should have followed him, but the way he walked away hurt so much she couldn't move. She could barely breathe. Not because she'd angered him over a mistake, but because he was so cool. So distant. So deliberate and so sure that he wanted her gone. As if their evenings at the tavern hadn't happened, as if all those stolen moments—that kiss—had meant nothing, he was tossing her out of his life.

Tears stung her eyes. The pain that gripped her hurt like a physical ache.

But common sense weaved its way into her thoughts. Why was she taking this personally? She didn't love him. She barely knew him. She had a fiancé—almost. A guy who might not be romantic, but who was certainly stable. She'd be going home in a little over two weeks. There could be nothing between her and Rafe. He was passion wrapped in electricity. Moody. Talented. Sweet but intense. Too sexy for his own good—or hers. And they weren't supposed to be attracted to each other, but they were.

Staying at Mancini's had been like tempting fate. Teasing both of them with something they couldn't have. Making them tense, and him moody. Hot one minute and cold the next.

So maybe it really was time to go?

She slammed the stack of menus into their shelf of the podium, grabbed her purse and raced out.

When she arrived at the villa, Louisa was on a ladder, staring at the watermarks as if she could divine how they got there.

"What are you doing home?"

Dani yanked the pins holding up her short curls and let them fall to her chin, as she kicked off Louisa's high, high heels.

"I was fired."

Louisa climbed off the ladder. "What?" She shook her head. "He told you to dress like the authority in the dining room and you were gorgeous. How could he not like how you looked?"

"Oh, I think he liked how I looked." Dani sucked in a breath, fully aware now that that was the problem. They were playing with fire. They liked each other. But neither of them wanted to. And she was done with it.

"Come to Rome with me."

"You're not going to try to get your job back?"

"It just all fell into place in my head. Rafe and I are attracted, but my boyfriend asked me to marry him. Though I didn't accept, I can't really be flirting with another guy. So Rafe—"

Louisa drew in a quick breath. "You know, I wasn't going to mention this because it's not my business, but now that you brought it up… Don't you think it's kind of telling that you hopped on a plane to Italy rather than accept your boyfriend's proposal?"

"I already had this trip scheduled."

"Do you love this guy?"

Dani hesitated, thinking of her last conversation with Paul and how he'd ordered her not to call him anymore. The real kicker wasn't his demand. It was that it hadn't affected her. She didn't miss their short, irrelevant conversations. In six months, she hadn't really missed *him*.

Oh, God. That was the thing her easy, intense attraction to Rafe was really pointing out. Her relationship to Paul might provide a measure of security, but she didn't love him.

She fell to a kitchen chair.

"Oh, sweetie. If you didn't jump up and down for joy when this guy proposed, and you find yourself attracted to another man, you do not want to accept that proposal."

Dani slumped even further in her seat. "I know."

"You should go back to Mancini's and tell Rafe that."

She shook her head fiercely. "No. *No!* He's way too much for me. Too intense. Too *everything*. He has me working twelve-hour days when I'm supposed to be on holiday finding my foster mother's relatives, enjoying some time with them before I go home."

"You're leaving me?"

Dani raised her eyes to meet Louisa's. "You've always known I was only here for a month. I have just over two weeks left. I need to start looking for the Felice family now." She smiled hopefully because she suddenly, fervently didn't want to be alone, didn't want the thoughts about Rafe that would undoubtedly haunt her now that she knew she couldn't accept Paul's proposal. "Come with me."

"To Rome?"

"You need a break from studying everything that's wrong with the villa. I have to pay for a room anyway. We can share it. Then we can come back and I'll still have time to help you catalog everything that needs to be fixed."

Louisa's face saddened. "And then you'll catch a plane and be gone for good."

Dani rose. "Not for good." She caught Louisa's hands. "We're friends. You'll stay with me when you have to come back to the States. I'll visit you here in Italy."

Louisa laughed. "I really could use a break from staring at so many things that need repairing and trying to figure out how I'm going to get it all done."

"So it's set. Let's pack now and go."

Within an hour, they were at the bus station. With Mancini's and Rafe off the list of conversation topics, they chit-chatted about the scenery that passed by as their bus made its way to Rome. Watching Louisa take it all in, as if trying to memorize the country in which she now owned property, a weird sense enveloped Dani. It was clear that everything was new, unique to Louisa. But it all seemed familiar to Dani, as if she knew the trees and grass and chilly February hills, and when she returned to the US she would miss them.

Which was preposterous. She was a New York girl. She needed the opportunities a big city provided. She'd never lived in the country. So why did every tree, every landmark, every winding road seem to fill a need inside her?

The feeling followed her to Rome. To the alleyways between the quaint buildings. To the sidewalk cafés and bistros. To the Colosseum, museums and fountains she took Louisa to see.

And suddenly the feeling named itself. *Home.* What she felt on every country road, at every landmark, gazing at every blue, blue sky and grassy hill was the sense that she was home.

She squeezed her eyes shut. She told herself she wasn't home. She was merely familiar with Italy now because she'd lived in Rome for months. Though that made her feel better for a few minutes, eventually she realized that being familiar with Rome didn't explain why she'd felt she belonged at Mancini's.

She shoved that thought away. She did not belong at Mancini's.

The next day, Dani and Louisa found Rosa's family and were invited to supper. The five-course meal began, reminding her of Rafe, of his big, elaborate dinners, the waitresses who were becoming her friends, the customers who loved her.The weepy sense that she had lost her home filled her. Rightly or wrongly, she'd become attached to Mancini's, but Rafe had fired her.

She had lost the place where she felt strong and smart and capable. The place where she was making friends who felt like family. The place where she—no matter how un-wise—was falling for a guy who made her breath stutter and her knees weak.

Because the guy she felt so much for had fired her.

Her brave facade fell away and she excused herself. In the bathroom, she slid down the wall and let herself cry. She'd never been so confused in her life.

"Rafe, there's a customer who'd like to talk to you."

Rafe set down his knife and walked to Mila, who stood in front of the door that led to the dining room. "Great, let's go."

Pleased to be getting a compliment, he reached around

Mila and pushed open the door for her. Since Dani had gone, compliments had been fewer and farther between. He needed the boost.

Mila paused by a table with two twentysomething American girls. Wearing thick sweaters and tight jeans, they couldn't hide their tiny figures. Or their ages. Too old for college and too young to have amassed their own fortunes, they appeared to be the daughters of wealthy men, in Europe, spending their daddies' money. Undoubtedly, they'd heard of him. Bored and perhaps interested in playing with a celebrity chef, they might be looking for some fun. If he handled this right, one of them could be sharing Chianti with him that night.

Ignoring the tweak of a reminder of sharing that wine with Dani, her favorite, he smiled broadly. "What can I do for you ladies?"

"Your ravioli sucked."

That certainly was not what he'd expected.

He bowed slightly, having learned a thing or two from his former hostess. He ignored the sadness that shot through him at even the thought of her, and said, "Allow me to cover your bill."

"Cover our bill?" The tiny blonde lifted a ravioli with her fork and let it plop to her plate. "You should pay us for enduring even a bite of this drivel."

The dough of that ravioli had serenaded his palms as he worked it. The sweet sauce had kissed his tongue. The problem wasn't his food but the palates of the diners.

Still, remembering Dani, he held his temper as he gently reached down and took the biceps of the blonde. "My apologies." He subtly guided her toward the door. The woman was totally cooperative until they got to the podium, and then she squirmed as if he was hurting her, and made a hideous face. Her friend snapped a picture with her phone.

"Get it on Instagram!" the blonde said as they raced out the door. "Rafe Mancini sinks to new lows!"

Furious, Rafe ran after them, but they jumped into their car and peeled out of his parking lot before he could catch them.

After a few well-aimed curses, he counted to forty. Great. Just when he thought rumors of his temper had died, two spoiled little girls were about to resurrect them.

He returned to the quiet dining room. Taking another page from Dani's book, he said, "I'm sorry for the disturbance. Everyone, please, enjoy your meals."

A few diners glanced down. One woman winced. A couple or two pretended to be deep in conversation, as if trying to avoid his misery.

With a weak smile, he walked into the kitchen, over to his workstation and picked up a knife.

Emory scrambled over and whispered, "You're going to have to find her."

Facing the wall, so no one could see, Rafe squeezed his eyes shut. He didn't have to ask who *her* was. The shifts Daniella had been gone had been awful. This was their first encounter with someone trying to lure out his temper, but there had been other problems. Squabbles among the waitresses. Seating mishaps. Lost reservations.

"Things are going wrong, falling through the cracks," Emory continued.

"This is my restaurant. I will find and fix mistakes."

"No. If there's anything Dani taught us, it's that you're a chef. You are a businessman, yes. But you are not the guy who should be in the dining room. You are the guy who should be trotted out for compliments. You are the special chef made more special by the fact that you must be enticed out to the dining room."

He laughed, recognizing he liked the sound of that because he did like to feel special. Or maybe he liked feeling that his food was special.

"Did you ever stop to think that you don't have a temper with the customers or the staff when Dani's around?"

He didn't even try to deny it. With the exception of being on edge because of his attraction to her, his temperament had improved considerably. "Yes."

Emory chuckled as if surprised by his easy acquiescence. "Because she does the tasks that you aren't made to do, which frees you up to do the things you like to do. So, let's just bring her back."

Missing Dani was about so, so much more than Emory knew. Not just a loss of menial tasks but a comfort level. It was as if she brought sunshine into the room. Into his life. But she was engaged.

"Why should I go after her?" Rafe finally faced Emory. "She is returning to America in two weeks."

"Maybe we can persuade her to stay?"

He sniffed a laugh. Leaning down so that only Emory would hear, he said, "She has a fiancé in New York."

Emory's features twisted into a scowl. "And she's in Italy? For months? Without him? Doesn't sound like much of a fiancé to me."

That brought Rafe up short. There was no way in hell he'd let the woman he loved stay alone in Italy for *months*. Especially not if the woman he loved was Daniella.

He didn't tell Emory that. His reasoning was mixed up in feelings that he wasn't supposed to have. He'd gone the route of a relationship once. He'd given up apprenticeships to please Kamila. Which meant he'd given up his dream for her. And still they hadn't made it.

But he'd learned a lesson. Relationships only put the future of his restaurants at stake, so he satisfied himself with one-night stands.

Dani would not be a one-night stand.

But Mancini's really wasn't fine without her.

And Mancini's was his dream. He needed Daniella at his restaurant way too much to break his own rule about relationships. And that was the real bottom line. Getting involved with her would risk his dream as much as Kamila had. He needed her as an employee and he needed to put everything else out of his mind.

Emory caught Rafe's arm. "Maybe there is an opportunity here. If she's truly unhappy, especially with her fiancé, you might be able to convince her Mancini's should be her new career."

That was exactly what Rafe intended to do.

"But you can't have that discussion over the phone. You need to go to Palazzo di Comparino tomorrow. Talk to her personally. Make your case. Offer her money."

"Okay. I'll be out tomorrow morning, maybe all day if I need the time. You handle things while I'm gone."

Emory grinned. "That's my boy."

At the crack of dawn the next morning, Louisa woke Dani and said she was ready to take the bus back to Monte Calanetti. She was happy to have met Dani's foster mom's relatives, but she was nervous, antsy about Palazzo di Comparino. It was time to go back.

After grabbing coffee at a nearby bistro, Dani walked her friend to the bus station, then spent the day with her foster mother's family. By late afternoon, she left, also restless. Like Louisa, she'd loved meeting the Felice family, but they weren't *her* family. Her family was the little group of restaurant workers at Mancini's.

Saddened, she began the walk back to her hotel. A block before she reached it, she passed the bistro again. Though the day was crisp, it was sunny. Warm in the rays that poured down on a little table near the sidewalk, she sat.

She ordered coffee, telling herself it wasn't odd that she felt a connection to the staff at Mancini's. They were nice people. Personable. Passionate. Of course, she felt as if they were family. She'd mothered the waitresses, babied the customers and fallen for Emory like a favorite uncle.

But she'd never see any of them again. She'd been fired

from Mancini's. Rafe hated her. She wouldn't go home happy, satisfied to have met Rosa's relatives, because the connection she'd made had been to a totally different set of people. She would board her plane depressed. Saddened. Returning to a man who didn't even want to pick her up at the airport. A man whose marriage proposal she was going to have to refuse.

A street vendor caught her arm and handed her a red rose.

Surprised, she looked at him, then the rose, then back at him again. "*Grazie...* I think."

He grinned. "It's not from me. It's from that gentleman over there." He pointed behind him.

Dani's eyes widened when she saw Rafe leaning against a lamppost. Wearing jeans, a tight T-shirt and the waist-length black wool coat that he'd worn to the tavern, he looked sexy. But also alone. Very alone. The way she felt in the pit of her stomach when she thought about going back to New York.

Her gaze fell to the rose. Red. For passion. But with someone like Rafe who was a bundle of passion about his restaurant, about his food, about his customers, the color choice could mean anything.

Carrying the rose, she got up from her seat and walked over to him. "How did you find me?"

"Would you believe I guessed where you were?"

"That would have to be a very lucky guess."

He sighed. "I talked to your roommate, Louisa, this afternoon. She told me where you were staying, and I drove to Rome. Walking to your hotel, I saw you here, having coffee."

He glanced away. "Look, can we talk?" He shoved his hands tightly into the side pockets of his coat and returned his gaze to hers. "We've missed you."

"We?"

She almost cursed herself for the question. But she

needed to hear him say it so she'd know she wasn't crazy, getting feelings for a guy who found it so easy to fire her.

"*I've* missed you." He sighed. "Two trust-fund babies faked me out the other night. They insulted my food and when they couldn't get a rise out of me, they made it look like I was tossing one out on her ear to get a picture for Instagram."

She couldn't help it. She laughed. "Instagram?"

"It's the bane of my existence."

"But you hadn't lost your temper?"

He shook his head and glanced away. "No. I hadn't." He looked back at her. "I remembered some things you'd done." He smiled. "I learned."

Her heart picked up at the knowledge that he'd learned from her, and the thrill that he was here, that he'd missed her. "You're not a bad guy."

His face twisted around a smile he clearly tried to hide. "According to Emory, I'm just an overworked guy. And interviewing for a new maître d' isn't helping. Especially when no one I talk to fits. It's why I need you. You're the first person to take over the dining room well enough that I don't worry."

She counted to ten, breathlessly waiting for him to expand on that. When he didn't, she said, "And that's all it is?"

"I know you want there to be something romantic between us. But there are things that separate us. Not just your fiancé, but my temperament. Really? Could you see yourself happy with me? Or when you look at me, do you see a man who takes what he wants and walks away? Because that's the man I really am. I put my restaurant first. I have no time for a relationship."

Her heart wept at what he said. But her sensible self, the lonely foster child who didn't trust the wash of feelings that raced through her every time she got within two feet of him, understood. He was a gorgeous man, born for the limelight, looking to make a name for himself. She was a foster kid, looking for a home. Peace. Quiet. Security. They might be physically attracted, but, emotionally, they were totally wrong for each other. No matter how drawn she was to him, she knew the truth as well as he did.

"You can't commit?"

He shook his head. "My commitment is to Mancini's. To my career. My reputation. I want to be one of Europe's famed chefs. Mancini's is my stepping stone. I do not have time for what other men want. A woman on their arm. Fancy parties. Marriage. To me those are irrelevant. All I want is success. So I would hurt you. And I don't want to hurt you."

"Which makes anything between us just business?"

"Just business."

Her job at Mancini's had awakened feelings in Dani she'd never experienced. Self-worth. A sense of place. An unshakable belief that she belonged there. And the click of connection that made her feel she had a home. Something deep inside her needed Mancini's. But she wouldn't go back only to be fired again.

"And you need me?"

He rolled his eyes. "You Americans. Why must you be showered with accolades?"

Oh, he did love to be gruff.

She slid her hand into the crook of his elbow and pointed to her table at the bistro. "I don't need accolades. I need acknowledgment of my place at Mancini's...and my coffee. I'm freezing."

He pulled his arm away from her hand and wrapped it around her shoulders. She knew he meant it only as a gesture between friends, but she felt his warmth seep through to her. Longing tugged at her heart. A fierce yearning that clung and wouldn't let go.

"You should wear a heavier coat."

His voice was soft, intimate, sending the feeling of rightness through her again.

"It was warm when I came here."

"And now it is cold. So from here on I will make sure you wear a bigger coat." He paused. His head tilted. "Maybe you need me, too?"

She did. But not in the way he thought. She wanted him to love her. Really love her. But to be the man of her dreams, he would have to be different. To be warm and loving. To want her—

And he might. Today. But he'd warned her that anything he felt for her was temporary. He couldn't commit. He didn't want to commit. And unless she wanted to get her heart broken, she had to really hear what he was saying. If she was going to get the opportunity to go back to the first place in her life that felt like home, Mancini's, and the first people who genuinely felt like family, his staff, then a romance between them had to be out of the question.

"I need Mancini's. I like it there. I like the people."

"Ah. So we agree."

"I guess. All I know for sure is that I don't want to go back to New York yet."

He laughed. They reached her table and he pulled out her chair for her. "That doesn't speak well of your fiancé."

Hauling in a breath, she sat, but she said nothing. Her stretching of the truth to Rafe about Paul being her fiancé sat in her stomach like a brick. Still, even though she knew she was going to reject his marriage proposal, it protected her and Rafe. Rafe wouldn't go after another man's woman. Not even for a fling. And he was right. If they had a fling, she would be crushed when he moved on.

One of his eyebrows rose, as he waited for her reply.

She decided they needed her stretched truth. But she couldn't out-and-out lie. "All right. Paul is not the perfect guy."

"I'm not trying to ruin your relationship. I simply believe you should think all of this through. You have a place here in Italy. Mancini's needs you. I would like for you to stay in Italy and work for me permanently, and if you decide to, then maybe your fiancé should be coming here."

She laughed. Really? Paul move to Italy because of her? He wouldn't even drive to the airport for her.

Still, she didn't want Paul in the discussion of her returning to Mancini's. She'd already decided to refuse his proposal. If she stayed in Italy, it had to be for her reasons.

"I think we're getting ahead of ourselves. I have a few weeks before I have to make any decisions."

"Two weeks and two days."

"Yes."

He caught her hands. Kissed the knuckles. "So stay. Stay with me, Daniella. Be the face of Mancini's."

Her heart kicked against her ribs. The way he said "Stay with me, Daniella" froze her lungs, heated her blood. She glanced at the red rose sitting on the table, reminded herself it didn't mean anything but a way to break the ice when he found her. He wasn't asking her to stay for any reason other than her abilities in his restaurant. And she shouldn't want to stay for any reason other than the job. If she could prove herself in the next two weeks, she wouldn't be boarding a plane depressed. She wouldn't be boarding a plane at all. She'd be helping to run a thriving business. Her entire life would change.

She pulled her hands away. "I can't accept Louisa's hospitality forever. I need to be able to support myself. Hostessing doesn't pay much."

He growled.

She laughed. He was so strong and so handsome and so perfect that when he let his guard down and was himself, his real self, with her, everything inside her filled with crazy joy. And maybe if she just focused on making him her friend, a friend she could keep forever, working for him could be fun.

"I can't pay a hostess an exorbitant salary."

"So give me a title to justify the money."

He sighed. "A title?"

"Sure, something like general manager should warrant a raise big enough that I can afford my own place."

His eyes widened. "General manager?"

"Come on, Rafe. Let's get to the bottom line here. If things work out when we return to Mancini's, I'm going to be taking on a huge chunk of your work. I'm also going to be relocating to another *country*. You'll need to make it worth my while."

He shook his head. "Dear God, you are bossy."

"But I'm right."

He sighed. "Fine. But if you're getting that title, you will earn it."

She inclined her head. "Seems fair."

"You'll learn to order supplies, check deliveries, do the job of managing things Emory and I don't have time for."

"Makes perfect sense."

He sighed. His eyes narrowed. "Anything else?"

She laughed. "One more thing." Her laughter became a silly giggle when he scowled at her. "A ride back to Louisa's."

He rolled his eyes. "Yes. I will drive you back to Louisa's. If you wish, I will even help you find an apartment."

Leaving the rose, she stood and pushed away from the table. "You keep getting ahead of things. We have two weeks for me to figure out if staying at Mancini's is right for me." She turned to head back to the hotel to check out, but spun to face him again. "Were I you, I'd be on my best behavior."

The next morning, she called Paul. If staying in Italy was the rest of her life, the *real* rest of her life, she had to make things right.

"Do you know what time it is?"

She could hear the sleep in his voice and winced. "Yes. Sorry. But I wanted to catch you before work."

"That's fine."

She squeezed her eyes shut as she gathered her courage. It seemed so wrong to break up with someone over the phone and, yet, they'd barely spoken to each other in six months. This was the right thing to do.

"Look, Paul, I'm sorry to tell you this over the phone, but I can't accept your marriage proposal."

"What?"

She could almost picture him sitting up in bed, her bad news bringing him fully awake.

"I'm actually thinking of not coming back to New York at all, but staying in Italy."

"What? What about your job?"

"I have a new job."

"Where?"

"At a restaurant."

"So you're leaving teaching to be a waitress?"

"A hostess."

"Oh, there's a real step up."

"Actually, I'm general manager," she said, glad she'd talked Rafe into the title. She couldn't blame Paul for being confused or angry, and knew he deserved an honest explanation.

"And I love Italy. I feel like I belong here." She sucked in a breath. "We've barely talked in six months. I'm going to make a wild guess that you haven't even missed me. I think we were only together because it was convenient."

Another man's silence might have been interpreted as misery. Knowing Paul the way she did, she recognized it as more or less a confirmation that she was right.

"I'm sorry not to accept your proposal, but I'm very happy."

After a second, he said, "Okay, then. I'm glad."

The breath blew back into her lungs. "Really?"

"Yeah. I did think we'd make a good married couple,

but I knew when you didn't say yes immediately that you might have second thoughts."

"I'm sorry."

"Don't be sorry. This is just the way life works sometimes."

And that was her pragmatic Paul. His lack of emotion might have made her feel secure at one time, but now she knew she needed more.

They talked another minute and Dani disconnected the call, feeling as if a weight had been taken from her shoulders, only to have it quickly replaced by another one. She'd had to be fair to Paul, but now the only defense she'd have against Rafe's charms would be her own discipline and common sense.

She hoped that was enough.

CHAPTER NINE

HER RETURN TO the restaurant was as joyous as a celebration. Emory grinned. The waitresses fawned over her. The busboys grew red faced. The chefs breathed a sigh of relief.

Annoyance worked its way through Rafe. Not that he didn't want his staff to adore her. He did. That was why she was back. The problem was he couldn't stop reliving their meeting in Rome. He'd said everything that he'd wanted to say. That he'd missed her. That he wanted her back. But he'd kept it all in the context of business. He'd missed her help. He wanted her to become the face of Mancini's. He didn't want anything romantic with her because he didn't want to hurt her. He'd been all business. And it had worked.

But with her return playing out around him, his heart rumbled at the injustice. He hadn't lied when he said he didn't want her back for himself, that he didn't want something romantic between them. His fierce protection of Mancini's wouldn't let him get involved with an employee he needed. But here at the restaurant, with her looking so pretty, helping make his dream a reality, he just wanted to kiss her.

He reminded himself that she had a fiancé—

A fiancé she admitted was not the perfect guy.

Bah! That fiancé was supposed to be the key weapon in his arsenal of ways to keep himself away from her. Her admission that he wasn't perfect, even the fact that she was considering staying in Italy, called her whole engagement into question. And caused all his feelings for her to surface and swell.

She swept into the kitchen. Wearing a blue dress that highlighted her blue eyes and accented a figure so lush she was absolutely edible, she glided over to Emory. He took her hands and kissed the back of both.

"You look better than anything on the menu."

Rafe sucked in a breath, controlling the unwanted ripple of longing.

Dani unexpectedly stepped toward Emory, put her arms around him and hugged him. Emory closed his eyes as if to savor it, a smile lifted his lips.

Rafe's yearning intensified, but with it came a tidal wave of jealousy. He lowered his knife on an unsuspecting stalk of celery, chopping it with unnecessary force.

Dani faced him. "Why don't you give me the key and I'll open the front door for the lunch crowd?"

He rolled his gaze toward her slowly. Even as the businessman inside him cheered her return, the jealous man who was filled with need wondered if he wasn't trying to drive himself insane.

"Emory, give her your key."

The sous-chef instantly fished his key ring out of his pocket and dislodged the key for Mancini's. "Gladly."

"Don't be so joyful." He glanced at Dani again, at the soft yellow hair framing her face, her happy blue eyes. "Have a key made for yourself this afternoon and return Emory's to him."

She smiled. "Will do, boss."

She walked out of the kitchen, her high heels clicking on the tile floor, her bottom swaying with every step, all eyes of the kitchen staff watching her go.

Jealousy spewed through him. "Back to work!" he yelped, and everybody scrambled.

Emory sauntered over. "Something is wrong?"

He chopped the celery. "Everything is fine."

The sous-chef glanced at the door Dani had just walked through. "She's very happy to be back."

Rafe refused to answer that.

Emory turned to him again. "So did you talk her into staying? Is her fiancé joining her here? What's going on?"

Rafe chopped the celery. "I don't know."

"You don't know if she's staying?"

"She said her final two weeks here would be something like a trial run for her."

"Then we must be incredibly good to her."

"I gave her a raise, a title. If she doesn't like those, then we should be glad if she goes home to her *fiancé*." He all but spat the word *fiancé*, getting angrier by the moment, as he gave Dani everything she wanted but was denied everything he wanted.

Emory said, "I still say something is up with this fiancé of hers. If she didn't tell him she's considering staying in Italy, then there's trouble in paradise. If she did, and he isn't on the next flight to Florence, then I question his sanity."

Rafe laughed.

"Seriously, Rafe, has she talked to you about him? I just don't get an engaged vibe from her."

"Are you saying she's lying?"

Emory inclined his head. "I don't think she's lying as much as I think her fiancé might be a real dud, and her engagement as flat as a crepe."

Rafe said only, "Humph," but once again her statement that her fiancé wasn't the perfect guy rolled through his head.

"I only mention this because I think it works in our favor."

"How so?"

"If she's not really in love, if her fiancé doesn't really love her, we have the power of Italy on our side."

"To?"

"To coax her to stay. To seduce her away from a guy who doesn't deserve her."

Rafe chopped the celery. His dreams were filled with scenarios where he seduced Daniella. Except he had a feeling that kind of seducing wasn't what Emory meant.

"Somehow or another we have to be so good to her that she realizes what she has in New York isn't what she wants."

Sulking, Rafe scraped the celery into a bowl. Why did he have to be the one doing all the wooing? *He* was a catch. He wanted her eyelashes to flutter when he walked by and her eyes to warm with interest. He had some pride, too.

Emory shook his head. "Okay. Be stubborn. But you'll be sorry if some pasty office dweller from New York descends on us and scoops her back to America."

Rafe all but growled in frustration at the picture that formed in his head. Especially since she had said her fiancé wasn't perfect. Shouldn't a woman in love swoon for the man she's promised to marry?

Yes. Yes. She should.

Yet, here she was, considering staying. Not bringing her fiancé into the equation.

And he suddenly saw what Emory was saying.

She wasn't happy with her fiancé. She was searching for something. She'd gone to Rome looking for her foster mother's relatives—family! What Dani had been looking for in Rome was family! That was why she was getting so close to the staff at Mancini's.

Still, something was missing.

He tapped his index fingers against his lips, thinking, and when the answer came to him he smiled and turned to Emory. "I will need time off tomorrow."

Emory's face fell. "You're taking another day?"

"Just lunch. And Daniella will be out for lunch, too."

Emory caught his gaze. "Really?"

"Yes. Don't go thinking this is about funny business.

I'm taking her apartment hunting. Dani is a woman looking for a family. She thinks she's found it with us. But Mancini's isn't a home. It's a place of business. Once I help her get a house, somewhere to put down roots, it will all fall into place for her."

Rafe's first free minute, he called the real estate agent who'd sold him his penthouse. She told him she had some suitable listings in Monte Calanetti and he set up three appointments for Daniella.

When the lunch crowd cleared, he walked into the empty, quiet dining room.

Dani smiled as he approached. "You're not going to yell at me for not going home and costing you two hours' wages are you?"

"You are management now. I expect you here every hour the restaurant is open."

"Except my days off."

He groaned. "Except your days off. If you feel comfortable not being here two days every week, I am fine with it. But if something goes wrong, you will answer for it."

She laughed. "Whatever. I've been coaching Allegra. She'll be much better from here on out. No more catastrophes while I'm gone."

"Great. I've lined up three appointments for us tomorrow."

She turned from the podium. "With vendors?"

"With my friend who is a real estate agent."

"I told you we shouldn't get ahead of ourselves."

"Our market is tight. You must be on top of things to get a good place."

"I haven't—"

He interrupted her. "You haven't decided you're staying. I get that. But if you choose to stay, I don't want you panicking. Getting ahead of a problem is how a smart businessperson staves off disaster."

"Yeah, I know."

"Good. Tomorrow morning, Emory will take over lunch prep while you and I apartment hunt. We can be back for dinner."

Sun poured in through the huge window of the kitchen of the first unit Maria Salvetti showed Rafe and Dani the next morning. Unfortunately, cold air flowed in through the cracks between the window and the wall.

Dani eased her eyes away from the unwanted ventilation and watched as Rafe walked across a worn hardwood floor, his motorcycle boots clicking along, his jeans outlining an absolutely perfect behind and his black leather jacket, collar flipped up, giving him the look of a dangerous rebel.

For the second time that morning, she told herself she was grateful he'd been honest with her about his inability to commit. She didn't know a woman who wouldn't fall victim to his steel-gray eyes and his muscled body. She had to be strong. And her decision to stay at Mancini's had to be made for all the right reasons.

She faced Maria. "I'd have to fix this myself?"

"*Sì*. It is for sale. It is not a rental."

She turned to Rafe. "I wouldn't have time to work twelve-hour days and be my own general contractor."

"You could hire someone."

She winced as she ran her hand along the crack between the wall and window. "Oh, yeah? Just how big is my raise going to be?"

"Big enough."

She shook her head. "I still don't like it."

She also didn't like the second condo. She did have warm, fuzzy feelings for the old farmhouse a few miles away from the village, but that needed more work than the first condo she'd seen.

Maria's smile dipped a notch every time Dani rejected a prospective home. She'd tried to explain that she wasn't even sure she was staying in Italy, but Maria kept plugging along.

After Dani rejected the final option, Maria shook Rafe's hand, then Dani's and said, "I'll check our listings again and get back to you."

She slid into her car and Dani sighed, glad to be rid of her. Not that Maria wasn't nice, but with her decision about staying in Italy up in the air, looking for somewhere to live seemed premature. "Sorry."

"Don't apologize quite yet." He pulled his cell phone from his jacket and dialed a number. "Carlo, this is Rafe. Could you have a key for the empty condo at the front desk? *Grazie.*" He slipped his phone into his jacket again.

She frowned at him. "You have a place to show me?"

He headed for his SUV, motioning for her to follow him. "Actually, I thought Maria would have taken you to his apartment first. It's a newly renovated condo in my building."

She stopped walking. "*Your* building?" She might be smart enough to realize she and Rafe were a bad bet, but all along she'd acknowledged that their spending too much time together was tempting fate. Now he wanted them to live in the same building?

"After Emory, you are my most valued employee. A huge part of Mancini's success. We need to be available for each other. Plus, there would be two floors between us. It's not like we'd even run into each other."

She still hesitated. "Your building's that big?"

"No. I value my privacy that much." He sighed. "Seriously. Just come with me to see the place and you will understand."

Dani glanced around as she entered the renovated old building, Rafe behind her. Black-and-white block tiles were accented by red sofas and chairs in a lounge area of the lobby. The desk for the doorman sat discreetly in a corner.

Leaning over her shoulder, Rafe said, "My home is the penthouse."

His warm breath tickled her ear and desire poured through her. She almost turned and yelled at him for flirting with her. Instead, she squelched the feeling. He probably wasn't flirting with her. This was just who he was. Gorgeous. Sinfully sexy. And naturally flirtatious. If she really intended to stay in Italy and work for him, she had to get accustomed to him. As she'd realized after she'd spoken to Paul, she would need discipline and common sense to keep her sanity.

He pointed at the side-by-side elevators. "I don't use those, and you can't use them to get to my apartment."

His breath tiptoed to her neck and trickled down her spine. Still, she kept her expression neutral when she turned and put them face-to-face, so close she could see the little flecks of silver in his eyes.

Just as her reactions couldn't matter, how he looked—his sexy face, his smoky eyes—also had to be irrelevant. If she didn't put all this into perspective now, this temptation could rule her life. Or ruin her life.

She gave him her most professional smile. "And I'd be a few floors away?"

"Not just a few floors, but also a locked elevator."

Dangling the apartment key, he motioned for her to enter the elevator when it arrived. They rode up in silence. He unlocked the door to the available unit and she gasped.

"Oh, my God." She spun to face him. "I can afford this?"

He laughed. "Yes."

From the look of the lobby, she'd expected the apartment to be ultramodern. The kind of place she would have killed to have in New York. Black-and-white. Sharp, but sterile. Something cool and sophisticated for her and distant Paul.

But warm beiges and yellows covered these walls. The

kitchen area was cozy, with a granite-topped breakfast bar where she could put three stools.

She saw it filled with people. Louisa. Coworkers from Mancini's. And neighbors she'd meet who could become like a family.

She caught that thought before it could take root. Something about Italy always caused her to see things through rose-colored glasses, and if she didn't stop, she was going to end up making this choice before she knew for certain that she could work with Rafe as a friend or a business associate, and forget about trying for anything more.

She turned to Rafe again. "Don't make me want something I can't have."

"I already told you that you can afford it."

"I know."

"So why do you think you can't have it?"

It was exactly what she'd dreamed of as a child, but she couldn't let herself fall in love with it. Or let Rafe see just how drawn she was to this place. If he knew her weakness, he'd easily lure her into staying before she was sure it was the right thing to do.

She pointed at the kitchen, which managed to look cozy even with sleek stainless-steel appliances, dark cabinets and shiny surfaces. "It's awfully modern."

"So you want to go back to the farmhouse with the holes in the wall?"

"No." She turned away again, though she lovingly ran her hand along the granite countertop, imagining herself rolling out dough to make cut-out cookies. She'd paint them with sugary frosting and serve them to friends at Christmas. "I want a homey kitchen that smells like heaven."

"You have that at Mancini's."

"I want a big fat sofa with a matching chair that feels like it swallows you up when you sit in it."

"You can buy whatever furniture you want."

"I want to turn my thermostat down to fifty-eight at night so I can snuggle under thick covers."

He stared at her as if she were crazy. "And you can do that here."

"Maybe."

"Undoubtedly." He sighed. "You have an idealized vision of home."

"Most foster kids do."

He leaned his shoulder against the wall near the kitchen. His smoky eyes filled with curiosity. She wasn't surprised when he said, "You've never really told me about your life. You mentioned getting shuffled from foster home to foster home, but you never explained how you got into foster care in the first place."

She shrugged. Every time she thought about being six years old, or eight years old, or ten years old—shifted every few months to the house of a stranger, trying unsuccessfully to mingle with the other kids—a flash of rejection froze her heart. She was an adult before she'd realized no one had rejected her, per se. Each child was only protecting himself. They'd all been hurt. They were all afraid. Not connecting was how they coped.

Nonetheless, the memories of crying herself to sleep and longing for something better still guided her. It was why she believed she could keep her distance from Rafe. Common sense and a longing for stability directed her decisions. Along with a brutal truth. The world was a difficult place. She knew that because she'd lived it.

"There's not much to tell. My mom was a drug addict."

He winced.

"There's no sense sugarcoating it."

"Of course there is. Everyone sugarcoats his or her past. It's how we deal."

She turned to him again, surprised by the observation. She'd always believed living in truth kept her sane. He seemed to believe exactly the opposite.

"Yeah. What did you sugarcoat?"

"I tell you that I'm not a good bet as a romantic partner."

She sniffed a laugh.

"What I should have said is that I'm a real bastard."

She laughed again. "Seriously, Rafe. I got the message the first time. You want nothing romantic between us."

"Mancini's needs you and I am not on speaking terms with any woman I've ever dated. So I keep you for Mancini's."

She looked around at the apartment, unable to stop the warm feeling that flooded her when he said he would keep her. Still, he didn't mean it the way her heart took it. So, remembering to use her common sense, she focused her attention on the apartment, envisioning it decorated to her taste. The picture that formed had her wrestling with the urge to tell him to get his landlord on the line so she could make an offer—then she realized something amazing.

"You knew I'd love this."

He had the good graces to look sheepish. "I assumed you would."

"No assuming about it, you *knew*."

"All right, I knew you would love it."

She walked over to him, as the strangest thought formed in her head. Maybe it wouldn't take a genius to realize the way to entice a former foster child would be with a home. But no one had ever wanted her around enough to figure that out.

"How did you know?"

He shrugged. His strong shoulders lifted the black leather of his jacket and ruffled the curls of his long, dark hair. "It didn't take much to realize that you'd probably lost your sense of home when your foster mother died."

She caught his gaze. "So?"

"So, I think you came to Italy hoping to find it with her relatives."

"They're nice people."

"Yes, but you didn't feel a connection to Rosa's nice relatives. Yet, you keep coming back to Mancini's, because you did connect with us."

Her heart stuttered. Even her almost fiancé hadn't understood why she so desperately wanted to find Rosa's family. But Rafe, a guy who had known her a little over two weeks, a guy she'd had a slim few personal conversations with, had seen it.

He'd also hit the nail on the head about Mancini's. She felt they were her family. The only thing she didn't have here in Italy was an actual, physical home.

And he'd found her one.

He cared about her enough to want to please her, to satisfy needs she kept close to her heart.

Afraid of the direction of her thoughts, she turned away and walked into the master bedroom. Seeing the huge space, her eyebrows rose. "Wow. Nice."

Rafe was right behind her. "Are you changing the subject on me?"

She pivoted and faced him. He seemed genuinely clueless about what he was doing. Not just giving her everything she wanted, but caring about her. He was getting to know her—the real her—in a way no one else in her life ever had. And the urge to fall into his arms, confess her fears, her hopes, her longings, was so strong, she had to walk away from him. If she fell into his arms now, she'd never come out. Especially if he comforted her. God help her if he whispered anything romantic.

"I think we need to change the subject."

"Why?"

She walked over to him again. For fifty cents, she'd answer him. She'd put her arms around his neck and tell him he was falling for her. The things he did—searching her out in Rome, making her general manager, helping her find a home—those weren't things a boss did. No matter how much he believed he needed her as an employee, he also had feelings for her.

But he didn't see it.

And she didn't trust it. He'd said he was a bastard? What if he really was? What if he liked her now, but didn't tomorrow?

"Because I'm afraid. Every time I put down roots, it fails." She said the words slowly, clearly, so there'd be no misunderstanding. Rafe was a smart guy. If she stayed in Italy, shared the joy of making Mancini's successful, no matter how strong she was, how much discipline she had, how much common sense she used, there was a chance she'd fall in love with him.

And then what?

Would she hang around his restaurant desperate for crumbs of affection from a guy who slept with her, then moved on?

That would be an epic fail. The very thought made her ill.

Because she couldn't tell him that, she stuck with the safe areas. The things they could discuss.

"For as good as I am at Mancini's, I can see us having a blowout fight and you firing me again. And for as much as I like the waitstaff, I can see them getting new jobs and moving on. This decision comes with risks for me. I know enough not to pretend things will be perfect. But I have to have at least a little security."

"You and your security. Maybe to hell with security and focus on a little bit of happiness."

Oh, she would love to focus on being happy. Touring Italy with him, stolen kisses, nights of passion. But he'd told her that wasn't in the cards and she believed him. Somehow she had to stop herself from getting those kinds of thoughts every time he said something that fell out of business mode and tipped over into the personal. That would be the only way she could stay at Mancini's.

When she didn't answer, he sighed. "I don't think it's an accident you found Mancini's."

"Of course not. Nico sent me."

"I am not talking about Nico. I'm talking about destiny."

She laughed lightly and walked away from him. It was almost funny the way he used the words and phrases of a lover to lure her to a job. It was no wonder her thoughts always went in the wrong direction. He took her there. Thank God she had ahold of herself enough to see his words for what they were. A very passionate man trying to get his own way. To fight for her sanity, she would always have to stand up to him.

"Foster kids don't get destinies. We get the knowledge that we need to educate ourselves so we can have security. If you really want me to stay, let me come to the decision for the right reasons. Because if I stay, you are not getting rid of me. I will make Mancini's my home." She caught his gaze. "Are you prepared for that?"

CHAPTER TEN

WAS HE PREPARED for that?

What the hell kind of question was that for her to ask?

He caught her arm when she turned to walk away. "Of course, I'm prepared for that! Good God, woman, I drove to Rome to bring you back."

She shook her head with an enigmatic laugh. "Okay. Just don't say I didn't warn you."

He rolled his eyes heavenward. Women. Who could figure them out? "I am warned." He motioned to the door. "Come. I'll drive you back to Louisa's."

But by the time they reached Louisa's villa and he drove back to his condo to change for work, her strange statement had rattled around in his head and made him crazy. Was he prepared for her staying? Idiocy. He'd all but made her a partner in his business. He *wanted* her to stay.

He changed his clothes and headed to Mancini's. Walking into the kitchen, he tried to shove her words out of his head but they wouldn't go—until he found the staff in unexpectedly good spirits. Then his focus fell to their silly grins.

"What's going on?"

Emory turned from the prep table. "Have you seen today's issue of *Tuscany Review*?"

In all the confusion over Daniella, he'd forgotten that today was the day the tourist magazine came out. He snatched it from Emory's hands.

"Page twenty-nine."

He flicked through the pages, getting to the one he wanted, and there was a picture of Dani. So many tourists had snapped pictures that someone from the magazine could have come in and taken this one without anyone in the restaurant paying any mind.

He read the headline. "Mancini's gets a fresh start."

"Read the whole article. It's fantastic."

As he began to skim the words, Emory said, "There's mention of the new hostess being pretty and personable."

Rafe inclined his head. "She is both."

"And mention of your food without mention of your temper."

His gaze jerked up to Emory. "No kidding."

"No kidding. It's as if your temper didn't exist."

He pressed the magazine to his chest. "Thank God I went to Rome and brought her back."

Daniella pushed open the door. Dressed in a sheath the color of ripe apricots, she smiled as she walked toward Rafe and Emory. "I heard something about a magazine."

Rafe silently handed it to her.

She glanced down and laughed. "Well, look at me."

"Yes. Look at you." He wanted to pull her close and hug her, but he crossed his arms on his chest. The very fact that he wanted to hug her was proof he needed to keep his distance. Even forgetting about the fiancé she had back home, she needed security enough that he wouldn't tempt her away from finding it. Her staying had to be about Mancini's and her desire for a place, a home. He had to make sure she got what she wanted out of this deal—without breaking her heart. Because if he broke her heart, she'd leave. And everything they'd accomplished up to now would have been for nothing.

"You realize that even if every chef and busboy cycles out, and every waitress quits after university, Emory and I will always be here."

Emory grinned at Daniella. Rafe nudged him. "Stop behaving like one of the Three Stooges. This is serious for her."

She looked up from the magazine with a smile for Rafe. "Yes. I know you will always be here." Her smile grew. "Did you ever stop to think that maybe that's part of the problem?"

With that she walked out of the kitchen and Rafe shook his head.

"She talks in riddles." But deep down he knew what was happening. He'd told her they'd never become lovers. She had feelings for him. Hell, he had feelings for her, but he intended to fight them. He'd told her anything between them was wrong, so she had to be sure she could work with him knowing there'd never be anything between them.

And maybe that's what she meant about being prepared.

Lately, it seemed he was fighting his feelings as much as she was fighting hers.

Two nights later, as the dinner service began to slow down, Rafe stepped out into the dining room to see his friend Nico walking into Mancini's. Nico's eyes lit when he saw Dani standing at the podium.

"Look at you!" He took her hand and gave her a little twirl to let her show off another pretty blue dress that hugged her figure.

Jealousy rippled through Rafe, but he squelched it. He put her needs ahead of his because that served Mancini's needs. It was a litany he repeated at least four times a day. After her comment about him being part of the reason her decision was so difficult, he'd known he had to get himself in line or lose her.

As he walked out of the kitchen, he heard Nico say, "Rafe tells me you're working out marvelously."

She smiled sheepishly. "I can't imagine anyone not loving working here."

Rafe sucked in a happy breath. She loved working at Mancini's. He knew that, of course, but it was good to hear her say it. It felt normal to hear her say it. As if she knew she belonged here. Clearly, keeping his distance the past two days had worked. Mancini's was warm and happy. The way he'd always envisioned it.

"We don't have reservations," Nico said when Dani glanced at the computer screen.

She smiled. "No worries. The night's winding down. We have plenty of space."

Seeing him approach, Nico said, "And here's the chef now."

"Nico!" Rafe grabbed him and gave him a bear hug. "What brings you here?"

"I saw your ravioli on Instagram and decided I had to try it."

"Bah! Damned trust-fund babies. I should—" He stopped suddenly. Half-hidden behind Nico was Marianna Amatucci, Nico's sister, who'd been traveling for the past year. Short with wild curly hair and honey skin, she was the picture of a natural Italian beauty.

"Marianna!" He nudged Nico out of the way and hugged her, too, lifting her up to swing her around. Rafe hadn't even seen her to say hello in months. Having her here put another piece of normalcy back in his life.

She giggled when he plopped her to the floor again.

"Daniella," he said, one hand around Marianna's waist, the other clasped on Nico's shoulder. "These are my friends. Nico and his baby sister, Marianna. They get the best table in the house."

She smiled her understanding, grabbed two menus and led Nico and Marianna into the dining room. "This way."

Rafe stopped her. "Not *there*. I want them by my kitchen." He took the menus from her hands. "I want to spoil them."

Nico chuckled and caught Dani's gaze. "What he really means is use us for guinea pigs."

She laughed, her gaze meeting Nico's and her cheeks turning pink.

An unexpected thought exploded in Rafe's brain. He'd told Dani he wanted nothing romantic between them. Her fiancé was a dud. Nico was a good-looking man. And Dani was a beautiful, personable woman. If she stayed, at some point, Dani and Nico could become lovers.

His gut tightened.

Still, shouldn't he be glad if Nico was interested in Daniella and that interest caused her to stay?

Of course he should. What he wanted from Daniella was a face for his business. If Nico could help get her to stay, then Rafe should help him woo her.

"You are lucky the night is nearly over," Rafe said as he pulled out Marianna's chair. He handed the menus to them both.

Smiling warmly at Nico, Dani said, "Can I take your drink orders?"

Nico put his elbow on the table and his chin on his fist as he contemplated Daniella, as if she were a puzzle he was trying to figure out.

Thinking of Dani and Nico together was one thing. Seeing his friend's eyes on her was quite another. The horrible black syrup of jealously poured through Rafe's veins like hot wax.

Unable to endure it, he waved Daniella away. "Go. I will take his drink order. You're needed at the door. The night isn't quite over yet."

She gave Nico one last smile and headed to her post.

Happier with her away from Nico, Rafe listened to his friend's wine choice.

Marianna said, "Just water for me."

Rafe gaped at her. "You need wine."

She shook her head. "I need water."

Rafe's jaw dropped. "You cannot be an Italian and refuse wine with dinner."

Nico waved a hand. "It's not a big deal. She's been weird ever since she came home. Just bring her the water."

Rafe called Allegra over so she could get Nico's wine from the bar and Marianna's water. All the while, Dani walked customers from the podium, past Nico, who would watch her amble by.

Rafe sucked in a breath, not understanding the feelings rumbling through him. He wanted Daniella to stay. Nico might give her a reason to do just that. He could not romance her himself. Yet he couldn't bear to have his friend even look at her?

"Give me ten minutes and I will make you the happiest man alive."

Nico laughed, his eyes on Daniella. "I sincerely doubt you can do that with food."

Jealousy sputtered through Rafe again. "Get your mind out of the gutter and off my hostess!"

Nico's eyes narrowed. "Why? Are you staking a claim?"

Rafe's chest froze and he couldn't speak. But Marianna shook her head. "Men. Does it always have to be about sex with you?"

Nico laughed.

Rafe spun away, rushing into the kitchen, angry with Nico but angrier with himself. He should celebrate Nico potentially being a reason for Daniella to stay. Instead, he was filled with blistering-hot rage. Toward his friend. It was insane.

To make up for his unwanted anger, he put together the best meals he'd ever created. Unfortunately, it didn't take ten minutes. It took forty.

Allegra took out antipasto and soups while he worked. When he returned to the dining room, there were no more people at the door. All customers had been seated. Tables that emptied weren't being refilled. Anticipating going home, the busboys cheerfully cleared away dishes.

And Dani sat with Nico and Marianna.

Forcing himself to be friendly—happy—Rafe set the plates of food in front of Nico and his sister.

Marianna said, "Oh, that smells heavenly."

Nico nodded. "Impressive, Rafe."

Dani inhaled deeply. "Mmm…"

Nico grinned, scooped up some pasta and offered it to Dani. "Would you like a bite?"

"Oh, I'd love a bite!"

Nico smiled.

Unwanted jealousy and an odd proprietary instinct rushed through Rafe. Before Daniella could take the bite Nico offered, Rafe grabbed the back of her chair and yanked her away from the table.

"I want her to eat that meal later tonight."

Nico laughed. "Really? What is this? A special occasion?"

Rafe knew Nico meant that as a joke, but he suddenly felt like an idiot as if Nico had caught his jealousy. He straightened to his full six-foot height. "Not a special occasion, part of the process. She's eaten bits of food to get our flavor, but tonight I had planned on treating her to an entire dinner."

Dani turned around on her chair to catch his gaze. "Really?"

Oh, Lord.

Something soft and earthy trembled through him, replacing his jealousy and feelings of being caught, as if they had never existed. Trapped in the gaze of her blue eyes, he quietly said, "Yes."

She rose, putting them face-to-face. "A private dinner?"

He shrugged, but everything male inside him shimmered. After days of only working together, being on his best behavior, he couldn't deny how badly he wanted time alone with her. He didn't want Nico to woo her. *He* wanted to woo her.

"Yes. A private dinner."

She smiled.

His breath froze. She was happy to be alone with him? He'd warned her...yet she still wanted to be alone with him? And what of her fiancé?

He pivoted and returned to the kitchen, not sure what he was doing. But as he worked, he slowed his pace. He rejected ravioli, spaghetti Bolognese. Both were too simple. Too common—

If he was going to feed her an entire meal, it would be his best. Pride the likes of which he'd never felt before rose in him. Only the best for his Dani.

He stopped, his finger poised above a pot, ready to sprinkle a pinch of salt.

His Dani?

He squeezed his eyes shut. Dear God. This wasn't just an attraction. He was head over heels crazy for her.

Dani alternated between standing nervously by the podium and sitting with Nico and Marianna.

The dining room had all but emptied, yet she couldn't seem to settle. Her fluttery stomach had her wondering if she'd even be able to eat what Rafe prepared for her.

A private dinner.

She had no idea what it meant, but when he emerged from the kitchen and walked to Nico's table, her breath stalled. He'd removed his smock and stood before the Amatuccis in dark trousers and a white T-shirt that outlined his taut stomach. Tight cotton sleeves rimmed impressive biceps and Dani saw a tattoo she'd never noticed before.

"I trust you enjoyed your dinners."

Nico blotted his mouth with a napkin, then said, "Rafe, you truly are gifted."

Rafe bowed graciously.

"And, Marianna." When Rafe turned to see her half-eaten meal, he frowned. "Why you not eat?"

She smiled slightly. "You give everyone enough to feed an army. Half was plenty."

"You'll take the rest home?"

She nodded and Rafe motioned for Allegra to get her plate and put her food in a take-out container.

Rafe chatted with Nico, calmly, much more calmly than Dani felt, but the second Allegra returned with the take-out container, Marianna jumped from her seat.

"I need to get home. I don't know what's wrong with me tonight, but I'm exhausted."

Nico rose, too. "It is late. Dinner was something of an afterthought. I promised Marianna I'd get her back at a decent hour. But I knew you'd want to see her after her year away, Rafe."

Rafe kissed her hand. "Absolutely. I'm just sorry she's too tired for us to catch up."

Dani frowned. Nico's little sister didn't look tired. She looked pale. Biting her lower lip, Dani realized she'd only known one other person who'd looked that way—

Rafe waved her over. "Say good-night to Nico and his sister."

Keeping her observations to herself, Dani smiled. "Good night, Marianna."

Marianna returned her smile. "I'm sure we'll be seeing more of you since Nico loves Rafe's food."

Nico laughed, took both her hands and kissed them. "Good night, Daniella. Tell your roomie I said hello."

Daniella's face reddened. Louisa had been the topic of most of Nico's questions when she'd sat with him and his sister, but there was no way in hell she'd tell Louisa Nico had mentioned her. Still, she smiled. Every time she talked to Nico, she liked him more. Which only made Louisa's dislike all the more curious.

"Good night, Nico."

After helping Marianna with her coat, Rafe walked his friends to their car. Dani busied herself helping the waitresses finish dining room cleanup. She didn't see Rafe return, but when a half hour went by, she assumed he'd come in through the back door to the kitchen.

Of course, he could be talking to beautiful Marianna. She might be with her brother, but that brother was a friend of Rafe's. And Nico had said he wanted to bring Marianna to Mancini's because he knew Rafe would want to see her. They probably had all kinds of stories to reminisce about. Marianna might be too young to have been his first kiss, his first love, but she was an adult now. A beautiful woman.

Realizing how possible it was that Rafe might be interested in Marianna, Dani swayed, but she quickly calmed herself. If she decided to stay, watching him with other women would be part of her life. She had to get used to this. She had to get accustomed to seeing him flirt, seeing beautiful women like Marianna look at him with interest.

She tossed a chair to the table with a little more force than was necessary.

Gio frowned. "Are you okay?"

She smiled. "Yes. Perfect."

"If you're not okay, Allegra and I can finish."

"I'm fine." She forced her smile to grow bigger. "Just eager to be done for the night."

As they finished the dining room, Rafe walked out of the kitchen to the bar. He got a bottle of wine and two glasses. As their private dinner became a reality, Dani's stomach tightened.

She squeezed her eyes shut, scolding herself. The dinner might be private for no other reason than the restaurant would be closed. Rafe probably didn't want to be alone with her as much as he wanted her to eat a meal, as hostess, so she could get the real experience of dining at Mancini's.

The waitresses left. The kitchen light went out, indicating Emory and his staff had gone.

Only she and Rafe remained.

He faced her, pointed at a chair. "Sit."

Okay. That was about as far from romantic as a man could get. This "private" dinner wasn't about the two of them having time together. It was about a chef who wanted his hostess to know his food.

She walked over, noticing again how his tight T-shirt accented a strong chest and his neat-as-a-pin trousers gave him a professional look. But as she got closer, Louisa's high, high heels clicking on the tile floor, she saw his gaze skim the apricot dress. His eyes warmed with interest. His lips lifted into a slow smile.

And her stomach fell to the floor. *This* was why she'd never quite been able to talk herself out of her attraction to him. He was every bit as attracted to her. He might try to hide it. He might fight it tooth and nail. But he liked her as more than an employee.

She reached the chair. He pulled it out, offering the seat to her.

As she sat, her back met his hands still on the chair. Rivers of tingles flowed from the spot where they touched. Her breath shuddered in and stuttered out. Nerves filled her.

He stepped away. "We're skipping soup and salad, since it's late." All business, he sat on the chair next to hers. He lifted the metal cover first from her plate, then his own. "I present beef *brasato* with pappardelle and mint."

When the scent hit her, her mouth watered. All thoughts of attraction fled as her stomach rumbled greedily. She closed her eyes and savored the aroma.

"You like?"

Unable to help herself, she caught his gaze. "I'm amazed."

"Wait till you taste."

He smiled encouragingly. She picked up her fork, filled it with pasta and slid it into her mouth. Knowing he'd made this just for her, the ritual seemed very decadent, very sensual. Their eyes met as flavor exploded on her tongue.

"Oh, God."

He grinned. "Is good?"

"You know you don't even have to ask."

He sat back with a laugh. "I was top of my class. I trained both in Europe and the United States so I could ascertain the key to satisfying both palates." He smiled slowly. "I am a master."

She sliced off a bit of the beef. It was so good she had to hold back a groan. "No argument here."

"Wait till you taste my tiramisu."

"No salad but you made dessert?"

He leaned in, studied her. "Are you watching your weight?"

She shook her head. "No."

"Then prepare to be taken to a world of decadence."

She laughed, expecting him to pick up his fork and eat his own meal. Instead, he stayed perfectly still, his warm eyes on her.

"You like it when people go bananas over your food."

"Of course."

But that wasn't why he was studying her. There was a huge difference between pride in one's work and curiosity about an attraction and she knew that curiosity when she saw it.

She put down her fork, caught in his gaze, the moment. "What are we really doing here, Rafe?"

He shook his head. "I'm not sure."

"You aren't staring at me like someone who wants to make sure I like his food."

"You are beautiful."

Her heart shivered. Her eyes clung to his. She wanted him to have said that because he liked her, because he was ready to do something about it. But a romance between them would be a disaster. She'd be hurt. She'd have to leave Monte Calanetti. She could not take anything he said romantically.

Forking another bite of food, she casually said, "Beauty doesn't pay the rent."

His voice a mere whisper, he said, "Why do you tease me?"

Her face fell. "I don't tease you!"

"Of course, you do. Every day you dress more beautifully, but you don't talk to me."

"I'm smart enough to stay away when a guy warns me off."

"Yet you tell me I must be prepared for you to stay."

"Because you…" *Like me.* She almost said it. But his admitting he liked her would be nothing but trouble. He might like her in the moment, but he wouldn't like her forever. It was stupid to even have that discussion.

She steered them away from it. "Because if I stay, no more firing me. You're getting me permanently."

"You keep saying that as if I should be afraid." He slid his arm to the back of her chair. His fingers rose to toy with the blunt line of her chin-length hair. "But your staying is not a bad thing."

The wash of awareness roaring through her disagreed. If she fell in love with him, her staying would be a very bad thing. His touching her did not help matters. With his fingers brushing her hair, tickling her nape, she couldn't move…could barely breathe.

His hand shifted from her hairline and wrapped around the back of her neck so he could pull her closer. She told herself to resist. To be smart. But something in his eyes wouldn't let her. As she drew nearer, he leaned in. Their gazes held until his lips met hers, then her eyelids dropped. Her breathing stopped.

Warm and sweet, his lips brushed her, and she knew why she hadn't resisted. She so rarely got what she wanted in life that when tempted she couldn't say no. It might be wrong to want him, but she did.

His hand slid from her neck to her back, twisting her to

sit sideways on her chair. Her arms lifted slowly, her hands hesitantly went to his shoulders. Then he deepened the kiss and her mind went blank.

It wasn't so much the physical sensations that robbed her of thought but the fact that he kissed her. He finally, finally kissed her the way he had the night he'd walked her to her car.

When he thought she was free.

When he wanted there to be something between them.

The kiss went on and on. Her senses combined to create a flood of need so strong that something unexpected suddenly became clear. She was already in love with Rafe. She didn't have to worry that someday she might fall in love. Innocent and needy as she was, she had genuinely fallen in love—

And he was nowhere near in love with her.

He was strong and stubborn, set in his ways. He said he didn't do relationships. He said he didn't have time. He'd told her he hurt women. And if he hurt her, she'd never be able to work for him.

Did she want to risk this job for a fling?

To risk her new friends?

Did she want to be hurt?

Hadn't she been hurt, rejected enough in her life already?

She jerked away from him.

He pulled away slowly and ran his hand across his forehead. "Oh, my God. I am so sorry."

"Sorry?" She was steeped in desire sprinkled with a healthy dose of fear, so his apology didn't quite penetrate.

"I told you before. I do not steal other men's women."

"Oh." She squeezed her eyes shut. Paul was such a done deal for her that she'd taken him out of the equation. But Rafe didn't know that. For a second she debated keeping up the charade, if only to protect herself. But they had hit the point where that wasn't fair. She couldn't let Rafe go on thinking he was romancing another man's woman. Especially not when she had been such a willing participant.

She sucked in a breath, caught his gaze and quietly said, "I'm not engaged."

Rafe sat up in his chair. "What?"

She felt her cheeks redden. "I'm not engaged."

His face twisted with incredulity. "You *lied*?"

"No." She bounced from her seat and paced away. "Not really. My boyfriend had asked me to marry him. I told him I needed time to think about it. I was leaving for Italy anyway—"

He interrupted her as if confused. "So your boyfriend asked you to marry him and you ran away?"

She swallowed. "No. I inherited the money for a plane ticket to come here to find Rosa's relatives and I immediately tacked extra time onto my teaching tour. All that had been done before Paul proposed."

"So his proposal was a stopgap measure."

She frowned. "Excuse me?"

"Not able to keep you from going to Italy, he tied you to himself enough that you would feel guilty if you got involved with another man while you were away." He caught her gaze. "But it didn't work, did it?"

She closed her eyes. "No."

"It shouldn't have worked. It was a ploy. And you shouldn't feel guilty about anything that happened while you were here since you're really not engaged."

"Well, it doesn't matter anyway. I called him after we returned from Rome and officially rejected his proposal."

"You told him no?"

She nodded. "And told him I might be staying in Italy." She sucked in a breath. "He wished me luck."

Rafe sat back in his chair. "And so you are free." He combed his fingers through his hair. Laughed slightly.

The laugh kind of scared her. She'd taken away the one barrier she knew would protect her. All she had now to keep her from acting on her love for him was her willpower. Which she'd just proven wasn't very strong.

"I should go."

His gaze slowly met hers. "You haven't finished eating."

His soulful eyes held hers and her stomach jumped. Everything about him called to her on some level. He listened when she talked, appreciated her work at his restaurant… was blisteringly attracted to her.

What the hell would have happened if she hadn't broken that kiss? What would happen if she stayed, finished her meal, let them have more private time? With Paul gone as protection, would he seduce her? And if she resisted… what would she say? Another lie? *I don't like you? I'm not interested? I don't want to be hurt?*

The last wasn't a lie. And it would work. But she didn't want to say it. She didn't want to hear him tell her one more time that he couldn't commit. She didn't want this night to end on a rejection.

"I want to go home."

His eyes on her, he rose slowly. "Let's go, then. I will clean up in the morning."

Finally breaking eye contact, she walked to the front of Mancini's to get her coat. Her legs shook. Her breaths hurt. Not because she knew she was probably escaping making love, but because he really was going to hurt her one day.

CHAPTER ELEVEN

THE NEXT MORNING, Rafe was in the dining room when Dani used her key to unlock the front door and enter Mancini's. Around him, the waitresses and busboys busily set up tables. The wonderful aromas of his cooking filled the air. But when she walked in, Dani brought the real life to the restaurant. Dressed in a red sweater with a black skirt and knee-high boots, she was just the right combination of sexy and sweet.

And she'd rejected him the night before.

Even though she'd broken up with her man in America.

Without saying good morning, without as much as meeting her gaze, he turned on his heel and walked into the kitchen to the prep tables where he inspected the handiwork of two chefs.

He waved his hand over the rolled-out dough for a batch of ravioli. "This is good."

He tasted some sauce, inclined his head, indicating it was acceptable and headed for his workstation.

Emory scrambled over behind him. "Is Daniella here?"

"Yes." But even before Rafe could finish the thought, she pushed open the swinging doors to the kitchen and entered. She strolled to his prep table, cool and nonchalant as if nothing had happened between them.

But lots had happened between them. He'd kissed her. And she'd told him she didn't have a fiancé. Then she'd run. Rejecting him.

"Good morning."

He forced his gaze to hers. His eyes held hers for a beat before he said, "Good morning."

Emory caught her hands. "Did you enjoy your dinner?"

She laughed. "It was excellent." She met Rafe's gaze again. "Our chef is extraordinary."

His heart punched against his ribs. How could a man not take that as a compliment? She hadn't just eaten his food the night before. She'd returned his kiss with as much passion and fervor as he'd put into it.

Emory glowed. "This we know. And we count on you to make sure every customer knows."

"Oh, believe me. I've always been able to talk up the food from the bites you've given me. But eating an entire serving has seared the taste of perfection in my brain."

Emory grinned. "Great!"

"I think our real problem will be that I'll start stealing more bites and end up fat as a barrel."

Emory laughed but Rafe looked away, remembering his question from the night before. *Are you watching your weight?* One memory took him back to the scene, the mood, the moment. How nervous she'd seemed. How she'd jumped when his hand had brushed her back. How her jitters had disappeared while they were kissing and didn't return until they'd stopped.

Because she had to tell him about her fiancé.

She wasn't engaged.

She *had* responded to him.

Emory laughed. "Occupational hazard."

Her gaze ambled to Rafe's again. All they'd had the night before was a taste of what could be between them. Yes, he knew he'd warned her off. But she'd still kissed him. He'd given her plenty of time to move away, but she'd stayed. Knowing his terms—that he didn't want a relationship—she'd accepted his kiss.

With their gazes locked, she couldn't deny it. He could see the heat in her blue eyes.

"From here on out, when we create a new dish or perfect an old one," Emory continued, oblivious to the nonverbal conversation she and Rafe were having, "you will sample."

"I want her to have more than a sample."

The words sprang from him without any thought. But he wouldn't take them back. He no longer *wanted* an affair with her. He now *longed* for it, yearned for it in the depths of his being. And they were adults. They weren't kids. Love affairs were part of life. She might get hurt, or because they were both lovers and coworkers, she might actually understand him. His life. His time constraints. His passion for his dream—

She might be the perfect lover.

The truth of that rippled through him. It might not be smart to gamble with losing her, but he didn't think he'd lose her. In fact, he suddenly, passionately believed a long-term affair was the answer to their attraction.

"And I know more than a sample would be bad for me." She shifted her gaze to Emory before smiling and walking out of the kitchen.

Rafe shook his head and went back to his cooking. He had no idea if she was talking about his food or the subtle suggestion of an affair he'd made, but if she thought that little statement of hers was a deterrent, she was sadly mistaken.

Never in his life had he walked away from something he really wanted and this would not be an exception. Especially since he finally saw how perfect their situation could be.

Dani walked out of the kitchen and pressed her hand to her jumpy stomach. Those silver-gray eyes could get more across in one steamy look than most men could in foreplay.

To bolster her confidence, which had flagged again, she

reminded herself of her final thoughts as she'd fallen asleep the night before. Rafe was a mercurial man. Hot one minute. Cold the next. And for all she knew, he could seduce her one day and dump her the next. She needed security. Mancini's could be that security. She would not risk that for an affair. No matter how sexy his eyes were when he said it. How deep his voice.

She walked to the podium. Two couples awaited. She escorted them to a table. As the day wore on, customer after customer chatted with her about their tours or, if they were locals, their homes and families. The waitstaff laughed and joked with each other. The flow of people coming in and going out, eating, serving, clearing tables surrounded her, reminded her that *this* was why she wanted to stay in Italy, at Mancini's. Not for a man, a romance, but for a life. The kind of interesting, fun, exciting life she'd never thought she'd get.

She wanted this much more than she wanted a fling that ended in a broken heart and took away the job she loved.

At the end of the night, Emory came out with the white pay envelopes. He passed them around and smiled when he gave one to Dani. "This will be better than last time."

"So my raise is in here?"

"Yes." He nodded once and strode away.

Dani tucked the envelope into her skirt pocket and helped the waitresses with cleanup. When they were done, she grabbed her coat, not wanting to tempt fate by being the only remaining employee when Rafe came out of the kitchen.

She walked to her car, aware that Rafe's estimation of her worth sat by her hip, half afraid to open it. He had to value her enough to pay her well or she couldn't stay. She would not leave the security of her teaching job and an apartment she could afford, just to be scraping by in a foreign country, no matter how much she loved the area, its people and especially her job.

After driving the car into a space in Louisa's huge garage, Dani entered the house through the kitchen.

Louisa sat at the table, enjoying her usual cup of tea before bedtime. "How did it go? Was he nice? Was he romantic? Or did he ignore you?"

Dani slipped off her coat. "He hinted that we should have an affair."

"That's not good."

"Don't worry. I'm not letting him change the rules he made in Rome. He said that for us to work together there could be nothing between us." She sucked in a breath. "So he can't suddenly decide it's okay for us to have an affair."

Louisa studied her. "I think you're smart to keep it that way, but are you sure it's what you want?"

"Yes. Today customers reminded me of why I love this job. Between lunch and dinner, I worked with Emory to organize the schedule for ordering supplies and streamline it. He showed me a lot of the behind-the-scenes jobs it takes to make Mancini's work. Every new thing I see about running a restaurant seems second nature to me."

"And?"

"And, as I've thought all along, I have instincts for the business. This could be more than a job for me. It could be a real career. If Rafe wants to risk that by making a pass at me, I think I have the reasoning set in my head to tell him no."

Louisa's questioning expression turned into a look of joy. "So you're staying?"

"Actually—" she waved the envelope "—it all depends on what's in here. If my salary doesn't pay me enough for my own house or condo, plus food and spending money, I can't stay."

Louisa crossed her fingers for luck. "Here's hoping."

Dani shook her head. "You know, you're so good to me I want to stay just for our friendship."

Louise groaned. "Open the darned thing already!"

She sliced a knife across the top of the envelope. When she saw the amount of her deposit, she sat on the chair across from Louisa. "Oh, my God."

Louisa winced. "That bad?"

"It's about twice what I expected." She took a breath. "What's he doing?"

Louisa laughed. "Trying to keep you?"

"The amount is so high that it's actually insulting." She rose from her seat, grabbed her coat and headed for the door. "Half this check would have been sufficient to keep me. This amount? It's—offensive." Almost as if he was paying her to sleep with him. She couldn't bring herself to say the words to Louisa. But how coincidental was it that he'd dropped hints that he wanted to have an affair, then paid her more money than she was worth?

The insult of it vibrated through her. The nerve of that man!

"Where are you going?"

"To toss this back in his face."

Yanking open the kitchen door, she bounded out into the cold, cold garage. She jumped into the old car and headed back to Monte Calanetti, parking on a side street near the building where Rafe had shown her the almost-perfect condo.

But as she strode into the lobby, she remembered she needed a key to get into the elevator that would take her to the penthouse. Hoping to ask the doorman for help, she groaned when she saw the desk was empty.

Maybe she should take this as a sign that coming over here was a bad idea?

She sucked in a breath. No. Their situation was too personal to talk about at Mancini's. And she wanted to yell. She wanted to vent all her pent-up frustrations and maybe even throw a dish or two. She had to talk to him now. Alone.

She walked over to the desk and eyed the phone. Luckily, one of the marked buttons said Penthouse. She lifted the receiver and hit the button.

After only one ring, Rafe answered. "Hello?"

She sucked in a breath. "It's me. Daniella. I'm in your lobby and don't know how to get up to your penthouse."

"Pass the bank of elevators we used to get to the condo I showed you and turn right. I'll send my elevator down for you."

"Don't I need a key?"

"I'll set it to return. You just get in."

She did as he said, walking past the first set of elevators and turning to find the one for the penthouse. She stepped through the open doors and they swished closed behind her.

Riding up in the elevator with its modern gray geometric-print wallpaper and black slate floors, she was suddenly overwhelmed by something she hadn't considered, but should have guessed.

Rafe was a wealthy man.

Watching the doors open to an absolutely breathtaking home, she tried to wrap her brain around this new facet of Rafe Mancini. He wasn't just sexy, talented and mercurial. He was rich.

And she was about to yell at him? She, who'd always been poor? Always three paychecks away from homelessness? She'd never, ever considered that maybe the reason he didn't think anything permanent would happen between them might be because they were so different. They lived in two different countries. They had two different belief systems. And now she was seeing they came from two totally different worlds.

Rafe walked around a corner, holding two glasses of wine.

"Chianti." He handed one to her and motioned to the black leather sofa in front of a stacked stone fireplace in the sitting area.

Unable to help herself, she glanced around, trepidation filling her. Big windows in the back showcased the winking lights of the village. The black chairs around a long black dining room table had white upholstered backs and cushions. Plush geometric-patterned rugs sat on almost-black hardwood floors. The paintings on the pale gray walls looked ancient—valuable.

It was the home of a wealthy, wealthy man.

"Daniella?"

And maybe that's why he thought he could influence her with money? Because she came from nothing.

That made her even angrier.

She straightened her shoulders, caught his gaze. "Are you trying to buy me off?"

"Buy you off?"

"Get me to stop saying no to a relationship by bribing me with a big, fat salary?"

He laughed and fell to the black sofa. "Surely this is a first. An employee who complains about too much money." He shook his head with another laugh. "You said you wanted to be compensated for relocating. You said you wanted to be general manager. That is what a general manager makes."

"Oh." White-hot waves of heat suffused her. Up until this very second, everything that happened with reference to her job at Mancini's had been fun or challenging. He pushed. She pushed back. He wanted her for his restaurant. She made demands. But holding the check, hearing his explanation, everything took on a reality that had somehow eluded her. She was general manager of a restaurant. *This* was her salary.

He patted the sofa. "Come. Sit."

She took a few steps toward the sofa, but the lights of the village caught her attention and the feeling of being Alice in Wonderland swept through her.

"I never in my wildest dreams thought I'd make this much money."

"Well, teachers are notoriously underpaid in America, and though you'd studied a few things that might have steered you to a more lucrative profession, you chose to be a teacher."

Her head snapped up and she turned to face him. "How do you know?"

He batted a hand. "Do I look like an idiot? Not only did I do due diligence in investigating your work history, but also I took a look at your college transcripts. Do you really think I would have given you such an important job if you didn't have at least one university course in accounting?"

"No." Her gaze on him, she sat on the far edge of the sofa.

His voice became soft, indulgent. "Perhaps in the jumble of everything that's been happening I did not make myself clear. I've told you that I intend to be one of the most renowned chefs in Europe. I can't do that from one restaurant outside an obscure Tuscan village. My next restaurant will be in Rome. The next in Paris. The next in London. I will build slowly, but I will build."

"You'd leave Mancini's?" Oddly, the thought actually made her feel better.

"I will leave Mancini's in Tuscany when I move to Rome to build Mancini's Rome." He frowned. "I thought I told you this." His frown deepened. "I know for sure I told you that Mancini's was only a stepping stone."

"You might have mentioned it." But she'd forgotten. She forgot everything but her attraction to him when he was around. She'd accused him of using promotions to cover his feelings for her. But she'd used her feelings for him to block what was really going on with her job, and now, here she was, in a job so wonderful she thought she might faint from the joy of it.

"With you in place I can move to the next phase of my business plan. But there's a better reason for me to move on. You and I both worry that if we do something about our attraction, you will be hurt when it ends and Mancini's will lose you." He smiled. "So I fix."

"You fix?"

"I leave. Once I start my second restaurant, you will not have to deal with me on a day-to-day basis." His smile grew. "And we will understand each other because we'll both work in the same demanding profession. You will understand if I cancel plans at the last minute."

This time the heat that rained down on her had nothing to do with embarrassment. He'd really thought this through. Like a man willing to shift a few things because he liked her.

"Oh."

"There are catches."

Her gaze jumped to his. "Catches?"

"Yes. I will be using you for help creating the other restaurants. To scout sites. To hire staff. To teach them how to create our atmosphere. That is your real talent." He held her gaze. "That is also why your salary is so high. You are a big part of Mancini's success. You created that atmosphere. I want it not just in one restaurant, but all of them, and you will help me get it."

The foster child taught not to expect much out of life, the little girl who learned manners only by mimicking what she saw in school, the Italian tourist who borrowed Louisa's clothes and felt as though she was playing dress up every day she got ready for work, that girl quivered with happiness at the compliment.

The woman who'd been warned by him that he would hurt her struggled with fear.

"You didn't just create a great job for me. You cleared the way for us to have an affair."

Rafe sighed. "Why are you so surprised? You're beautiful. You're funny. You make me feel better about myself. My life. Yes, I want you. So I figured out a way I could have you."

She sucked in a breath. It was heady stuff to see the lengths he was willing to go to be with her. And she also saw the one thing he wasn't saying.

"You like me."

"What did you think? That I'd agonize this much over someone I just wanted to sleep with?"

She smiled. "You agonized?"

He batted a hand in dismissal. "You're a confusing woman, Daniella."

"And you've gone to some pretty great lengths to make sure we can…see each other."

His face turned down into his handsome pout. "And you should appreciate it."

She did. She just didn't know how to handle it.

"Is it so hard to believe I genuinely like you?"

"No." She just never expected he would say it. But he said it easily. And the day would probably come when those feelings would expand. He truly liked her and she was so in love with him that her head spun. This was not going to be an affair. He was talking about a relationship.

Happiness overwhelmed her and she couldn't resist. She set her wineglass on the coffee table and scooted beside him.

A warm, syrupy feeling slid through Rafe. But on its heels was the glorious ping of arousal. Before he realized what she was about to do, she kissed him. Quick and sweet, her lips met his. When she went to pull back, he slid his hand across her lower back and hauled her to him. He deepened their kiss, using his tongue to tempt her. Nibbling her lips. Opening his mouth over hers until she responded with the kind of passion he'd always known lived in her heart.

He pulled away. "You play with fire."

Her tongue darted out to moisten her lips. Temptation roared through him and all his good intentions to take it slowly with her melted like snow in April. He could have her now. In this minute. He could take what he greedily wanted.

She drew a breath. "How is it playing with fire if we really, really like each other?"

She was killing him. Sitting so warm and sweet beside him, tempting him with what he wanted before she was ready.

Still, though it pained him, he knew the right thing to do.

"So we will do this right. When you are ready, when you trust me, we will take the next step."

Her gaze held his. "When I trust you?"

"*Sì*. When I feel you trust me enough to understand why we can be lovers, you will come to my bed."

Her face scrunched as she seemed to think all that through. "Wait…this is just about becoming lovers?"

"Yes."

"But you just said you wouldn't worry that much about someone you wanted to sleep with." She caught his gaze. "You said you agonized."

"Because we will not be a one-night stand. We will be lovers. Besides, I told you. I don't do relationships."

"You also said that you'd never have a romance with an employee." She met his gaze. "But you changed that rule."

"I made accommodations. I made everything work."

"Not for me! I don't just want a fling! I want something that's going to last."

His eyebrows rose. "Something that will last?" He frowned. "Forever?"

"Forever!"

"I tried forever. It did not work for me."

"You tried?"

"*Sì.*"

"And?"

"And it ended badly." He couldn't bring himself to explain that he'd been shattered, that he'd almost given up his dream for a woman who had left him, that he'd been a ball of pain and confusion until he pulled himself together and realized his dreams depended on him not trusting another woman with his heart or so much of his life.

"*Cara*, marriage is for other people. It's full of all kinds of things incompatible with the man I have to be to be a success."

"You *never* want to get married?"

"No!" He tossed his hands. "What I have been saying all along? Do you not listen?"

She stood up. The pain on her face cut through him like a knife. Though he suddenly wondered why. He'd always known she wanted security. He'd always known he couldn't give it to her. He couldn't believe he'd actually tried to get her to accept less than what she needed.

He rose, too. "Okay, let's forget this conversation happened. It's been a long day. I'm tired. I also clearly misinterpreted things. Come to Mancini's tomorrow as general manager."

She took two steps back. "You're going to keep me, even though I won't sleep with you?"

"Yes." But the sadness that filled him confused him. He'd had other women tell him no and he'd walked away unconcerned. Her *no* felt like the last page of a favorite book, the end of something he didn't want to see end. And yet he knew she couldn't live with his terms and he couldn't live with hers.

CHAPTER TWELVE

AGREEING THAT HE was right about at least one thing—she was too tired, too spent, to continue this discussion—Dani walked to the elevator. He followed her, hit the button that would close the door and turned away.

She sucked in a breath and tried to still her hammering heart. But it was no use. They really couldn't find a middle ground. It was sweet that he'd tried, but it was just another painful reminder that she had fallen in love with the wrong man.

She squeezed her eyes shut. She'd be okay—

No, she wouldn't. She'd fallen in love with him. Unless he really stayed out of Mancini's, she'd always be in love with him. Then she'd spend her life wishing he could fall for her, too. Or maybe one day she'd succumb. She'd want him so much she'd forget everything else, and she'd start the affair he wanted. With the strength of her feelings, that would seal the deal for her. She'd love him forever. Then she'd never have a home. Never have a family. Always be alone.

She thought of the plane ticket tucked away somewhere in her bedroom in Louisa's house. Now that she knew he wanted nothing but an affair, which was unacceptable, she could go home.

But she didn't want to go home. She wanted to run Mancini's. He'd handed her the opportunity with her general managership—

And he was leaving. Maybe not permanently, but for the next several years he wouldn't be around every day. Most of the time, he'd be in other cities, opening new restaurants.

Wouldn't she be a fool to leave now? Especially since she had a few days before she had to use that ticket. Maybe the wise thing to do would be to use this time to figure out if she could handle working with him as the boss she only saw a few times a month?

The next day when she walked in the door and felt the usual surge of rightness, she knew the job was worth fighting for. In her wildest dreams she'd never envisioned herself successful. Competent, making a living, getting a decent apartment? Yes. But never as one of the people at the top. Hiring employees. Creating atmosphere. Would she really let some feelings, one *man*, steal this from her?

No! No! She'd been searching for something her entire life. She believed she'd found it at Mancini's. It would take more than unrequited love to scare her away from that.

When Emory sat down with her in between lunch and dinner and showed her the human resources software, more of the things she'd learned in her university classes tumbled back.

"So I'll be doing all the admin?"

Emory nodded. "With Rafe gone, setting up Mancini's Rome, I'll be doing all the cooking. I won't have time to help."

"That's fine." She studied the software on the screen, simple stuff, really. Basically, it would do the accounting for her. And the rest? It was all common sense. Ordering. Managing the dining room. Hiring staff.

He squeezed her hand. "You and me...we make a good team."

Her smile grew and her heart lightened. She loved Emory.

Even tempered with the staff and well acquainted with

Rafe's recipes, he was the perfect chef. As long as Rafe wasn't around, she would be living her dream.

She returned his hand squeeze. "Yeah. We do."

When she and Emory were nearly finished going over the software programs, Rafe walked into the office. As always when he was around, she tingled. But knowing this was one of the things she was going to have to deal with, because he wasn't going away permanently, she simply ignored it.

"Have you taught her payroll?"

Emory rose from his seat. "Yes. In fact, she explained a thing or two to me."

Rafe frowned. "How so?"

"She understands the software. I'm a chef. I do not."

Dani also rose from her chair. "I've worked with software before to record grades. Essentially, most spreadsheet programs run on the same type of system, the same theories. My boyfriend—" She stopped when the word *boyfriend* caught in her throat. Emory's gaze slid over to her. But Rafe's eyes narrowed.

She took a slow, calming breath. "My ex-boyfriend Paul is a computer genius. I picked up a few things from him."

Rafe turned away. "Well, let us be glad for him, then."

He said the words calmly, but Dani heard the tension in his voice. There were feelings there. Not just lust. So it wouldn't be only her own feelings she'd be fighting. She'd also have to be able to handle his. And that might be a little trickier.

"I've been in touch with a Realtor in Rome. I go to see buildings tomorrow."

A look passed between him and Emory.

Emory tucked the software manual into the bottom bin of an in basket. "Good. It's time to get your second restaurant up and running." He slid from behind the desk. "But right now I have to supervise dinner."

He scampered out of the room and Rafe's gaze roamed over to hers again. "I'd like for you to come to Rome with me."

Heat suffused her and her tongue stuck to the roof of her mouth. "Me?"

"I want you to help me scout locations."

"Really?"

"I told you. You are the one who created the atmosphere of this Mancini's. If I want to re-create it, I think you need to be in on choosing the site."

Because that made sense and because she did have to learn to deal with him as a boss, owner of the restaurant for which she worked, she tucked away any inappropriate longings and smiled. "Okay."

She could be all business because that's what really worked for them.

The next day, after walking through an old, run-down building with their Realtor, Rafe and Dani stepped out into the bright end-of-February day.

"I could do with a coffee right now."

He glanced at her. In her sapphire-blue coat and white mittens, she looked cuddly, huggable. And very, very, very off-limits. Her smiles had been cool. Her conversations stilted. But she'd warmed up a bit when they actually began looking at buildings.

"Haven't you already had two cups of coffee?"

She slid her hand into the crook of his elbow, like a friend or a cousin, someone allowed innocent, meaningless touches.

"Don't most Italians drink something like five cups a day?"

When he said, "Bah," she laughed.

All morning, their conversation at his apartment two nights ago had played over and over and over in his head. She wanted a commitment and he didn't. So he'd figured out a way they could be lovers and work together and she'd rejected it. He'd had to accept that.

But being with her this morning, without actually being allowed to touch her or even contemplate kissing her was making him think all kinds of insane things. Like how empty his life was. How much he would miss her when he stopped working at the original Mancini's and headquartered himself in Rome.

So though he knew her hand at his elbow meant nothing, he savored the simple gesture. It was a safe, nonthreatening way to touch her and have her touch him. Even if he did know it would lead to nothing.

"Besides, I love coffee. It makes me warm inside."

"True. And it is cold." He slid his arm around her shoulders. Her thick coat might keep her toasty, but it was another excuse to touch her.

They continued down the quiet street, but as they approached a shop specializing in infant clothing, the wheels of a baby stroller came flying out the door and straight for Daniella's leg. He caught her before she could as much as wobble and shifted her out of the way.

The apologetic mom said, *"Scusi!"*

Dani laughed. In flawless Italian she said, "No harm done." Then she bent and chucked the chin of the baby inside the stroller. "Isn't she adorable!"

The proud mom beamed. Rafe stole a quiet look at the kid and his lips involuntarily rose as a chuckle rumbled up from the deepest part of him. "She likes somebody's cooking."

The mom explained that the baby had her father's love of all things sweet, but Rafe's gaze stayed on the baby. She'd caught his eye and cooed at him, her voice a soft sound, almost a purr, and her eyes as shiny as a harvest moon.

A funny feeling invaded his chest.

Dani gave the baby a big, noisy kiss on the cheek, said

goodbye to the mom and took his arm so they could resume their walk down the street.

They ducked into a coffeehouse and she inhaled deeply. "Mmm...this reminds me of being back in the States."

He shook his head. "You Americans. You copy the idea of a coffeehouse from us, then come over here and act like we must meet your standards."

With a laugh, she ordered two cups of coffee, remembering his choice of brews from earlier that morning. She also ordered two scones.

"I hope you're hungry."

She shrugged out of her coat before sitting on the chair he pulled out for her at a table near a window. "I just need something to take the edge off my growling stomach. The second scone is for you."

"I don't eat pastries from a vendor who sells in bulk."

She pushed the second scone in front of him anyway. "Such a snob."

He laughed. "All right. Fine. I will taste." He bit into the thing and to his surprise it was very good. Even better with a sip or two of coffee. So tasty he ate the whole darned thing.

"Not quite the pastry snob anymore, are you?"

He sat back. He truly did not intend to pursue her. He respected her dreams, the way he respected his own. But that didn't stop his feelings for her. With his belly full of coffee and scone, and Daniella happy beside him, these quiet minutes suddenly felt like spun gold.

She glanced around. "I'll bet you've brought a woman or two here."

That broke the spell. "What?" He laughed as he shifted uncomfortably on his chair. "What makes you say that?"

"You're familiar with this coffeehouse. This street. You were even alert enough to pull me out of the way of the oncoming stroller at that baby shop." She shrugged. "You might not have come here precisely, but you've brought women to Rome."

"Every Italian man brings women to Rome." He toyed with his now-empty mug. He'd lived with Kamila just down the street. He'd dreamed of babies like the little girl in the stroller.

"I told you about Paul. I think you need to tell me about one of your women to even the score."

"You make me sound like I dated an army."

She tossed him an assessing look. "You might have."

Not about to lie, he drew a long breath and said, "There were many."

She grimaced. "Just pick one."

"Okay. How about Lisette?"

She put her elbow on the table, her eyes keen with interest. "Sounds French."

"She was."

"Ah."

"I met her when she was traveling through Italy…" But even as he spoke, he remembered that she was more driven than he was. *He* had taken second place to *her* career. At the time he hadn't minded, but remembering the situation correctly, he didn't feel bad about that breakup.

"So what happened?"

He waved a hand. "Nothing. She was just very married to her career."

"Like you?"

He laughed. "Two peas in a pod. But essentially we didn't have time for each other."

"You miss her?"

"No." He glanced up. "Honestly, I don't miss any of the women who came into and walked out of my life."

But he had missed Kamila and he would miss Dani if she left. He'd miss her insights at the restaurant and the way she made Mancini's come alive. But most of all he'd miss her smile. Miss the way she made *him* feel.

The unspoken truth sat between them. Their gazes caught, then clung. That was the problem with Dani. He felt for her the same things he had felt with Kamila. Except stronger. The emotions that raced through him had nothing to do with affairs, and everything to do with the kind of commitment he swore he'd never make again. That was why he'd worked so hard to figure out a way they could be together. It was why he also worked so hard to steer them away from a commitment. This woman, this Dani, was everything Kamila had been…and more.

And it only highlighted why he needed to be free.

He cleared his throat. "There was a woman."

Dani perked up.

"Kamila." He toyed with his mug again, realizing he was telling her about Kamila as much to remind himself as to explain to Dani. "She was sunshine when she was happy and a holy terror when she was not."

Dani laughed. "Sounds exciting."

He caught her gaze again. "It was perfect."

Her eyes softened with understanding. "Oh."

"You wonder how I know I'm not made for a relationship? Kamila taught me. First, she drew me away from my dream. To please her, I turned down apprenticeships. I took a permanent job as a sous-chef. I gave up the idea of being renowned and settled for being happy." Though it hurt, he held her gaze. "We talked about marriage. We talked about kids. And one day I came home from work and discovered her things were gone. *She* was gone. I'd given up everything for her and the life I thought I wanted, and she left without so much as an explanation of why."

"I'm sorry."

"Don't be." He sucked in a breath, pulled away from her, as his surety returned to him. "That loss taught me to be careful. But more than that it taught me never to do anything that jeopardizes who I am."

"So this Kamila really did a number on you."

"Were you not listening? There was no number. Yes, she broke my heart. But it taught me lessons. I'm fine."

"You're wounded." She caught his gaze. "Maybe even more wounded than I am."

He said, "That's absurd," but he felt the pangs of loss, the months of loneliness as if it were yesterday.

"At least I admit I need someone. You let one broken romance evolve into a belief that a few buildings and success are the answers to never being hurt. Do you think that when you're sixty you're going to look around and think 'I wish I'd started more Mancini's'? Or do you think you're going to envy your friends' relationships, wish for grandkids?"

"I told you I don't want those things." But even as he said the words, he knew they were a lie. Not a big pulsing lie, but a quiet whisper of doubt. Especially with the big eyes of the baby girl in the stroller pressed into his memory. With a world of work to do to get his chain of restaurants started, what she said should seem absurd. Instead, he saw himself old, his world done, his success unparalleled and his house empty.

He blinked away that foolish thought. He had family. He had friends. His life would never be empty. That was Dani's fear, not his.

"Let's go. Mario gave me the address of the next building where we're to meet him."

Quiet, they walked to his car, slid in and headed to the other side of the city. More residential than the site of the first property, this potential Mancini's had the look of a home, as did his old farmhouse outside Monte Calanetti.

He opened the door and she entered the aging building before him. Mario came over and shook his hand, but Dani walked to the far end of the huge, open first floor. She found the latch on the shutters that covered a big back window. When she flipped it, the shutters opened. Sunlight poured in.

Rafe actually *felt* the air change, the atmosphere shift. Though the building was empty and hollow, with her walking in, the sunlight pouring in through a back window, everything clicked.

This was his building. And she really was the person who brought life to his dining rooms. He'd had success of a sort without her, but she breathed the life into his vision, made it more, made it the vision he saw when he closed his eyes and dreamed.

Dani ambled to the center of the room. Pointing near the door, she said, "We'd put the bar over here."

He frowned. "Why not here?" He motioned to a far corner, out of the way.

"Not only can we give customers the chance to wait at the bar for their tables, but also we might get a little extra drink business." She smiled at him as she walked over. "Things will be just a tad different in a restaurant that's actually in a residential area of a city." Her smile grew. "But I think it could be fun to play around with it."

He crossed his arms on his chest to keep from touching her. He could almost feel the excitement radiating from her. While he envisioned a dining room, happy customers eating *his* food, he could tell she saw more. Much more. She saw things he couldn't bring into existence because all he cared about was the food.

"What would you play around with?"

Her gaze circled the room. "I'm not sure. We'd want to keep the atmosphere we've build up in Mancini's, but here we'd also have to become part of the community. You can get some really great customer relations by being involved with your neighbors." She tapped her finger on her lips. "I'll need to think about this."

Rafe's business instincts kicked in. He didn't know what she planned to do, but he did know whatever she decided, it would probably be good. Really good. Because she had the other half of the gift he'd been given.

He also knew she was happy. Happier than he'd ever seen her. Her blue eyes lit with joy. Her shoulders were back. Her steps purposeful. Confidence radiated from her.

"You want Mancini's to be successful as much as I want it to be successful."

She laughed. "I doubt that. But I do want it to be the best it can be." She glanced around, then faced him again. "In all the confusion between us, I don't think I've ever said thank-you."

"You wish to thank me?"

"For the job. For the fun of it." She shrugged. "I need this. I don't show it often but deep down inside me, there's a little girl who always wondered where she'd end up. *She* needed the chance to be successful. To prove her worth."

He smiled. "She'll certainly get that with Mancini's."

"And we're going to have a good time whipping this into shape."

He smiled. "That's the plan."

Her face glowed. "Good."

He said, "Good," but his voice quieted, his heart stilled, as he suddenly realized something he should have all along. Kamila had broken his heart. But Dani had wheedled her way into his soul. His dream.

If he and Dani got close and things didn't work out, he wouldn't just spend a month drinking himself silly. He'd lose everything.

CHAPTER THIRTEEN

THE NEXT DAY in the parking lot of Mancini's, Dani switched off the ignition of Louisa's little car, knowing that she was two days away from D-day. Decision day. The day she had to use her return ticket to New York City.

Being with Rafe in Rome had shown her he respected her opinion. Oh, hell, who was she kidding? Telling her about Kamila had been his way of putting the final nail in the coffin of her relationship dreams. It hurt, but she understood. In fact, in a way she was even glad. Now that she knew why he was so determined, she could filter her feelings for him away from her longing for a relationship with him and into his dream. He needed her opinion. He wanted to focus on food, on pleasing customer palates. She saw the ninety thousand other things that had to be taken care of. Granted, he'd chosen a great spot for the initial Mancini's. He'd fixed the building to perfection. But a restaurant in the city came with different challenges.

Having lived in New York and eaten at several different kinds of restaurants, she saw things from a customer's point of view. And she knew exactly how she'd set up Mancini's Rome restaurant.

She *knew.*

The confidence of it made her forget all about returning to New York, and stand tall. She entered the kitchen on her way to the office, carrying a satchel filled with pictures she'd printed off the internet the night before using Louisa's laptop.

This was her destiny.

Then she saw Rafe entering through the back door and her heart tumbled. He wore the black leather jacket. He hadn't pulled his hair into the tie yet and it curled around his collar. His eyes were cool, serious. When their gazes met, she swore she could feel the weight of his sadness.

She didn't understand what the hell he had to be sad about. He was getting everything he wanted. Except her heart. He didn't know that he already had her love, but their good trip the day before proved they could work together, even be friends, and he should appreciate that.

Everything would be perfect, as long as he didn't kiss her. Or tempt her. And yesterday he'd all but proven he needed her too much to risk losing her.

"I have pictures of things I'd like your opinion on."

Emory looked from one to the other. "Pictures?"

Rafe slowly ambled into the kitchen. "Dani has ideas for the restaurant in Rome."

Emory gaped at him. "Who cares? You have a hundred-person wedding tomorrow afternoon."

Dani's mouth fell open. Rafe's eyes widened. "We didn't cancel that?"

"We couldn't," Emory replied before Dani said anything, obviously taking the heat for it. "So I called the bride's mother yesterday and got the specifics. Tomorrow morning, we'll all come here early to get the food prepared. In the afternoon Dani and I will go to the wedding. I will watch your food, Chef Mancini. Your reputation will not suffer."

Rafe slowly walked over to Dani. "You know we cannot do this again!"

"Come on, Chef Rafe." She smiled slightly, hoping to dispel the tension, again confused over why he was so moody. "Put Mr. Mean Chef away. I got the message the day you fired me over this." With that she strode into the office, dumped her satchel on the desk and swung out again. She thought of the plane ticket in her pocket and reminded herself that in two days she wouldn't have that option. When he yelled, she'd have to handle it.

"I'll be in the dining room, checking with Allegra on how things went yesterday."

Rafe sagged with defeat as she stormed out. He shouldn't have yelled at her again about the catering, but everything in his life was spinning out of control. He saw babies in his sleep and woke up hugging his pillow, dreaming he was hugging Daniella. The logical part of him insisted they were a team, that a real relationship would enhance everything they did. They would own Mancini's together, build it together, build a life together.

The other part, the part that remembered Kamila, could only see disaster when the relationship ended. When Kamila left, he could return to his dream. If Dani left, she took half of his dream with her.

He faced Emory. "I appreciate how you have handled this. And I apologize for exploding." He sucked in a breath. "As penance, I will go to the wedding tomorrow."

Emory laughed. "If you're expecting me to argue, you're wrong. I don't want to be a caterer, either."

"As I said, this is penance."

"Then you really should be apologizing to Dani. It was her you screamed at."

He glanced at the door as he shrugged out of his jacket. She was too upset with him now. And she was busy. He would find a minute at the end of the night to apologize for his temper. If he was opting out of a romance because he needed her, he couldn't lose her over his temper.

But she didn't hang around after work that night. And the next morning, he couldn't apologize because they weren't alone. First, he'd cooked with a full staff. Then he'd had to bring Laz and Gino, two of the busboys, to the wedding to assist with setup and teardown. They drove to the vineyard in almost complete silence, every mile stretching Rafe's nerves.

Seeing the sign for 88 Vineyards, he turned down the winding lane. The top of a white tent shimmered in the winter sun. Thirty yards away, white folding chairs created two wide rows of seating for guests. He could see the bride and groom standing in front of the clergyman, holding hands, probably saying their vows.

He pulled the SUV beside the tent. "It looks like we'll need to move quickly to get everything set up for them to eat."

Dani opened her door of the SUV. "Not if there are pictures. I've known brides who've taken hours of pictures."

"Bah. Nonsense."

Ignoring him, she climbed out of the SUV.

Rafe opened his door and recessional music swelled around him. Still Dani said nothing. Her cold shoulder stung more than he wanted to admit.

A quick glance at the wedding ceremony netted him the sight of the bride and groom coming down the aisle. The sun cast them in a golden glow, but their smiles were even more radiant. He watched as the groom brought the bride's hand to his lips. Saw the worship in his eyes, the happiness, and immediately Rafe thought of Daniella. About the times he'd kissed her hand. Walked her to her car. Waited with bated breath for her arrival every morning.

He reached into his SUV to retrieve a tray of his signature ravioli. Handing it to Laz, he sneaked a peek at Daniella as she made her way to the parents of the bride, who'd walked out behind the happy couple. They smiled at her, the bride's mom talking a million words a second as she pointed inside the tent. Daniella set her hand on the mom's forearm and suddenly the nervous woman calmed.

He watched in heart-stealing silence. A lifetime of rejection had taught her to be kind. And one failed romance had made him mean. Bitter.

As he pulled out the second ravioli tray, Dani walked over.

"Apparently the ceremony was lovely."

"Peachy."

"Come on. I know you're mad at me for arranging this. But at the time, I didn't know any better and in a few hours all of this will be over."

He sucked in a breath. "I'm not mad at you. I'm angry with myself—" *Because I finally understand I'm not worried about you leaving me, or even losing my dreams. I'm disappointed in myself*"—for yelling at you yesterday."

"Oh." She smiled slowly. "Thanks."

The warm feeling he always got when she smiled invaded every inch of him. "You're welcome."

Not waiting for him to say anything else, she headed inside the white tent where the dinner and reception would be held. He followed her only to discover she was busy setting up the table for the food. He and Laz worked their magic on the warmers he'd brought to keep everything the perfect temperature. Daniella and Gino brought in the remaining food.

And nothing happened.

People milled around the tables in the tent, chatting, celebrating the marriage. Wine flowed from fancy bottles. The mother of the bride socialized. The parents of the groom walked from table to table. A breeze billowed around the tent as everyone talked and laughed.

He stepped outside, nervous now. He'd never considered himself wrong, except that he'd believed giving up apprenticeships for Kamila had made him weak. But setback after setback had made Dani strong. It was humbling to realize his master-chef act wasn't a sign of strength, but selfishness. Even more humbling to realize he didn't know what to do with the realization.

Wishing he still smoked, he ambled around the grounds, gazing at the blue sky, and then he turned to walk down a cobblestone path, only to find himself three feet away from the love-struck bride and groom.

He almost groaned, until he noticed the groom lift the bride's chin and tell her that everything was going to be okay.

His eyebrows rose. They hadn't even been married twenty minutes and there was trouble in paradise already?

She quietly said, "Everything is not going to be okay. My parents are getting a divorce."

Rafe thought of the woman in pink, standing with the guy in the tux as they'd chatted with Dani at the end of the ceremony, and he almost couldn't believe it.

The groom shook his head. "And they're both on their best behavior. Everything's fine."

"For now. What will I do when we get home from our honeymoon? I'll have to choose between the two of them for Christmas and Easter." She gasped. "I'll have to get all my stuff out of their house before they sell it." She sucked in a breath. "Oh, my God." Her eyes filled with tears. "I have no home."

Rafe's chest tightened. He heard every emotion Dani must feel in the bride's voice. No home. No place to call her own.

A thousand emotions buffeted him, but for the first time since he'd met Dani he suddenly felt what she felt. The emptiness of belonging to no one. The longing for a place to call her own. And he realized the insult he'd leveled when he'd told her he wanted to sleep with her, but not keep her.

"I'll be your home." The groom pulled his bride away from the tree. "It's us now. We'll make your home."

We'll make your home.

Rafe stepped back, away from the tree that hid him, the words vibrating through him. But the words themselves were nothing without the certainty behind them.

The strength of conviction in the groom's voice. The promise that wouldn't be broken.

We'll make your home.

"Let's go inside. We have a wedding to celebrate."

She smiled. "Yes. We do."

Rafe discreetly followed them into the tent. He watched them walk to the main table as if nothing was wrong, as the dining room staff scrambled to fill serving bowls with his food and get it onto tables.

The toast of the best man was short. Rafe's eyes strayed to Daniella. He desperately wanted to give her a home. A real one. A home like he'd grown up in with kids and a dog and noisy suppers.

This was what life had stolen from her and from him. When Kamila left, she hadn't taken his dream. She'd bruised him so badly, he'd lost his faith in real love. He'd lost his dream of a house and kids. And when it all suddenly popped up in the form of a woman so beautiful that she stole his breath, he hadn't seen it.

Dear God. He loved her. He loved her enough to give up everything he wanted, even Mancini's, to make her dreams come true. But he wouldn't have to give up anything. His dream was her dream. And her dream was now his dream.

Their meal eaten, the bride and groom rose from the table. The seating area was quickly dismantled by vineyard staff, who left a circle of chairs around the tent and a clear floor on which to dance.

The band introduced the bride and groom and he took her hand and kissed it before he led her in their dance.

Emotion choked Rafe. He'd spent the past years believing the best way to live his dream was to hold himself back, forget love, when the truth was he simply needed to meet the right woman to realize his dream would be hollow, empty without her.

"Hey." Daniella walked up beside him. "Dinner is

over. We can dismantle our warmers, take our trays and go home."

He faced her. Emotions churned inside him. Feelings for Dani that took root and held on. He'd found his one. He'd fired her, yelled at her, asked her to become his lover. And she'd held her ground. Stood up to him. Refused him. Forced him to work by her terms. And she had won him.

But he had absolutely no idea how to tell her that.

She picked up an empty tray and headed for his SUV. Grabbing up another empty tray, he scurried after her.

"I've been thinking about our choice."

She slid the tray into the SUV. "Our choice?"

"You know. Our choice not to—"

Before he could finish, the busboys came out of the tent with more trays. Frustration stiffened his back. With a quick glance at him, Dani walked back to the noisy reception for more pans. The busboys got the warmers.

Simmering with the need to talk, Rafe silently packed it all inside the back of his SUV.

Nerves filled him as he drove his empty pans, warmers and employees to Mancini's. When they arrived, the restaurant bustled with diners. Emory raced around the kitchen like a madman. Daniella pitched in to help Allegra. Rafe put on his smock, washed his hands and helped Emory.

Time flew, as it always did when he was busy, but Rafe kept watching Daniella. Something was on her mind. She smiled. She worked. She teased with staff. But he heard something in her voice. A catch? No it was more of an easing back. The click of connection he always heard when she spoke with staff was missing. It was as if she were distancing herself—

Oh, dear God.

In all the hustle and bustle that had taken place in the past four weeks, she'd never made the commitment to stay.

And she had a plane ticket for the following morning.

The night wound down. Emory headed for the office to

do some paperwork. Rafe casually ambled into the dining room. As the last of the waitstaff left, he pulled a bottle of Chianti from the rack and walked around the bar to a stool.

He watched Dani pause at the podium, as if torn between reaching for her coat and joining him. His heart chugged. Everything inside him froze.

Finally, she turned to him. Her lips lifted into a warm smile and she sashayed over.

Interpreting her coming to him as a good sign, he didn't give himself time to think twice. He caught her hands, lifted both to his lips and said, "Pick me."

Her brow furrowed. "What?"

"I know you're thinking about leaving. I see it on your face. Hear it in your voice. I know you think you have nothing here but a job, but that's not true. I need you for so much more. So pick me. Do not work for me. Pick me. Keep me. Take *me*."

Her breath hitched. "You're asking me to quit?"

"No." He licked his suddenly dry lips. He'd known this woman only twenty-four days. Yet what he felt was stronger than anything he'd ever felt before.

"Daniella, I think I want you to marry me."

Dani's heart bounced to a stop as she yanked her hands out of his.

"What?"

"I want you to marry me."

She couldn't stop the thrill that raced through her, but even through her shock she'd heard his words clearly. "You said *think*. You said you *think* you want to marry me."

He laughed a bit as he pulled his hand through his hair. "It's so fast for me. My God, I never even thought I'd want to get married. Now I can't imagine my life without you." He caught her hand again, caught her gaze. "Marry me."

His voice had become stronger. His conviction obvious.

"Oh." She wanted to say yes so bad it hurt to wrestle the

word back down her throat. But she had to. "For a month you've said you don't do relationships. Now suddenly you want to marry me?"

He laughed. "All these years, I thought I was weak because I gave Kamila what she wanted and she left me anyway. So I made myself strong. People saw me as selfish. I thought I was determined."

"I understand that."

"Now I see I *was* selfish. I did not want to lose my dream again."

"I understand that, too."

He shook his head fiercely. "You're missing what I'm telling you. I might have been broken by her loss, but Kamila was the wrong woman for me. I was never my real self with her. I was one compromise after another. With you, I am me. I see my temper and I rein it back. I see myself with kids. I see a house. I long to make you happy."

Oh, dear God, did the man have no heart? "Don't say things you don't mean."

"I never say things I don't mean. I love you, Daniella." He reached for her again. "Do not get on that plane tomorrow."

She stepped back, so far that he couldn't touch her, and pressed her fingers to her lips. Her heart so very desperately wanted to believe every word he said. Her brain had been around, though, for every time that same heart was broken. This man had called Paul's proposal a stopgap measure...yet, here he was doing the same thing.

"No."

His face fell. "No?"

"What did you tell me about Paul asking to marry me the day before I left New York?"

He frowned.

"You said it was a stopgap measure. A way to keep me." He walked toward her. "Daniella..."

She halted him with a wave of her hand. "Don't. I feel

foolish enough already. You're afraid I'm going to go home so you make a proposal that mocks everything I believe in."

She yearned to close her eyes at the horrible sense of how little he thought of her, but she held them open, held back her tears and made the hardest decision of her life.

"I'm going back to New York." Her heart splintered in two as she realized this really was the end. They'd never bump into each other at a coffee shop, never sit beside each other in the subway, never accidentally go to the same dry cleaner. He lived thousands of miles away from her and there'd be no chance for them to have the time they needed to really fall in love. He'd robbed them of that with his insulting proposal.

"Mancini's will be fine without me." She tried a smile. "*You* will be fine without me." She took another few steps back. "I've gotta go."

CHAPTER FOURTEEN

DANI RACED OUT of Mancini's, quickly started Louisa's little car and headed home. Her flight didn't leave until ten in the morning. But she had to pack. She had to say goodbye to Louisa. She had to give back the tons of clothes her new friend had let her borrow for her job at Mancini's.

She swiped at a tear as she turned down the lane to Palazzo di Comparino. Her brain told her she was smart to be going home. Her splintered heart reminded her she didn't have a home. No one to return to in the United States. No one to stay for in Italy.

The kitchen light was on and as was their practice, Louisa had waited up for Dani. As soon as she stepped in the kitchen door, Louisa handed her a cup of tea. Dani glanced up at her, knowing the sheen of tears sparkled on her eyelashes.

"What's wrong?"

"I'm going home."

Louisa blinked. "I thought this was settled."

"Nothing's ever settled with Rafe." She sucked in a breath. "The smart thing for me is to leave."

"What about the restaurant, your job, your destiny?"

She fell to a seat. "He asked me to marry him."

Louisa's eyes widened. "How is that bad? My God, Dani, even I can see you love the guy."

"I said no."

"Oh, sweetie! Sweetie! You love the guy. How the hell could you say no?"

"I've been here four weeks, Louisa. Rafe is a confirmed bachelor and he asked me to marry him. The day before I'm supposed to go home. You do the math."

"What math? You have a return ticket to the United States. He doesn't want you to go."

Dani slowly raised her eyes to meet Louisa's. "Exactly. The proposal was a stopgap measure. He told me all about it when we talked about Paul asking me to marry him. He said Paul didn't want to risk losing me, so the day before I left for Italy, he'd asked me to marry him."

"And you think that's what Rafe did?"

Her chin lifted. "You don't?"

Rafe was seated at the bar on his third shot of whiskey when Emory ambled out into the dining room.

"What are you doing here?"

He presented the shot glass. "What does it look like I'm doing?"

Emory frowned. "Getting drunk?"

Rafe saluted his correct answer.

"After a successful catering event that could have gone south, you're drinking?"

"I asked Daniella to marry me. And do you know what she told me?"

Looking totally confused, Emory slid onto the stool beside Rafe. "Obviously, she said no."

"She said no."

Emory laughed. Rafe scowled at him. "Why do you think this is funny?"

"The look on your face is funny."

"Thanks."

"Come on, Rafe, you've known the girl a month."

"So she doesn't trust me?"

Emory laughed. "Look at you. Look at how you've treated her. Would you trust you?"

"Yeah, well, she's leaving for New York tomorrow. I didn't want her to go."

Emory frowned. "Ah. So you asked her to marry you to keep her from going?"

"No. I asked her to marry me because I love her." He rubbed his hand along the back of his neck. "But I'd also told her that her boyfriend had asked her to marry him the day before she left for Italy as a stopgap measure. Wanting to tie her to him, without giving her a real commitment, he'd asked. But he hadn't really meant it. He just didn't want her to go."

Emory swatted him with a dish towel. "Why do you tell her these things?"

"At the time it made sense."

"Yeah, well, now she thinks you only asked her to marry you to keep her from going back to New York."

"No kidding."

Emory swatted him again. "Get the hell over to Palazzo di Comparino and fix this!"

"How?"

Emory's eyes narrowed. "You know what she wants... what she needs. Not just truth, proof. If you love her, and you'd better if you asked her to marry you, you have to give her proof."

He jumped off the stool, grabbed Emory's shoulders and noisily kissed the top of his head. "Yes. Yes! Proof! You are a hundred percent correct."

"You just make sure she doesn't get on that plane."

Dani's tears dried as she and Louisa packed her things. Neither one of them expected to sleep, so they spent the night talking. They talked of keeping in touch. Video chatting and texting made that much easier than it used to be. And

Louisa had promised to come to New York. They would be thousands of miles apart but they would be close.

Around five in the morning, Dani shoved off her kitchen chair and sadly made her way to the shower. She dressed in her own old raggedy jeans and a worn sweater, the glamour of her life in Tuscany, and Louisa's clothes behind her now.

When she came downstairs, Louisa had also dressed. She'd promised to take her to the airport and she'd gotten ready.

But there was an odd gleam in her eye when she said, "Shall we go?"

Dani sighed, knowing she'd miss this house but also realizing she'd found a friend who could be like a sister. The trip wasn't an entire waste after all.

She smiled at Louisa. "Yeah. Let's go."

They got into the ugly green car and rather than let Dani drive, Louisa got behind the wheel.

"I thought you refused to drive until you understood Italy's rules of the road better."

Stepping on the gas, Louisa shrugged. "I've gotta learn some time."

She drove them out of the vineyard and out of the village. Then the slow drive to Florence began. But even before they went a mile, Louisa turned down an old road.

"What are you doing?"

"I promised someone a favor."

Dani frowned. "Do we have time?"

"Plenty of time. You're fine."

"I know I'm fine. It's my flight I'm worried about."

"I promise you. I will pull into the driveway and be pulling out two minutes later."

Dani opened her mouth to answer but she snapped it closed when she realized they were at the old farmhouse Maria the real estate agent had shown her and Rafe. She faced Louisa. "Do you know the person who bought this?"

"Yes." She popped open her door. "Come in with me."

Dani pushed on her door. "I thought you said this would only take a minute."

"I said two minutes. What I actually said was I promise I will be pulling out of this driveway two minutes after I pull in."

Dani walked up the familiar path to the familiar door and sighed when it groaned as Louisa opened it. "Whoever bought this is in for about three years of renovations."

Louisa laughed before she called out, "Hello. We're here."

Rafe stepped out from behind a crumbling wall. Dani skittered back. "Louisa! *This* is your friend?"

"I didn't say he was my friend. I said I knew him." Louisa gave Dani's back a little shove. "He has some important things to say to you."

"I bought this house for you," Rafe said, not giving Dani a chance to reply to Louisa.

"I don't want a house."

He sighed. "Too bad. Because you now have a house." He motioned her forward. "I see a big kitchen here. Something that smells like heaven."

She stopped.

He motioned toward the huge room in the front. "And big, fat chairs that you can sink into in here."

"Very funny."

"I am not being funny. You," he said, pointing at her, "want a home. I want you. Therefore, I give you a home."

"What? Since a marriage proposal didn't keep me, you offer me a house?"

"I didn't say I was giving you a house. I said I was giving you a home." He walked toward the kitchen. "And you're going to marry me."

She scrambled after him. "Exactly how do you expect to make that happen?"

She rounded the turn and walked right into him. He caught her arms and hauled her to him, kissing her. She made a token protest, but, honestly, this was the man she couldn't resist.

He broke the kiss slowly, as if he didn't ever want to have to stop kissing her. "That's how I expect to make that happen."

"You're going to kiss me until I agree?"

"It's an idea with merit. But it won't be all kissing. We have a restaurant. You have a job. And there's a bedroom back here." He headed toward it.

Once again, she found herself running after him. Cold air leeched in from the window and she stopped dead in her tracks. "The window leaks."

"Then you're going to have to hire a general contractor."

"Me?"

He straightened to his full six-foot-three height. "I am a master. I cook."

"Oh, and I clean and make babies?"

He laughed. "We will hire someone to clean. Though I like the part about you making babies."

Her heart about pounded its way out of her chest. "You want kids?"

He walked toward her slowly. "*We* want kids. We want all that stuff you said about fat chairs and good-smelling kitchens and turning the thermostat down so that we can snuggle."

Her heart melted. "You don't look like a snuggler."

"I'll talk you into doing more than snuggling."

She laughed. Pieces of the ice around her heart began to melt. Her eyes clung to his. "You're serious?"

"I wouldn't have told Louisa to bring you here if I weren't. I don't do stupid things. I do impulsive things." He grinned. "You might have to get used to that."

She smiled. He motioned for her to come closer and when she did, he wrapped his arms around her.

"I could not bear to see you go."

"You said Paul only asked me to marry him as a stop-gap measure."

"Yes, but Paul is an idiot. I am not."

She laughed again and it felt so good that she paused to revel in it. To memorize the feeling of his arms around her. To glance around at their house.

"Oh, my God, this is a mess."

"We'll be fine."

She laid her head on his chest and breathed in his scent. She counted to ten, waited for him to say something that would drive her away, then realized what she was really waiting for.

She glanced up at him. "I'm so afraid you're going to hurt me."

"I know. And I'm going to spend our entire lives proving to you that you have no need to worry."

She laughed and sank against him again. "I love you."

"After only four weeks?"

She peeked up again. "Yes."

"So this time you'll believe me when I say it."

She swallowed. Years of fear faded away. "Yes."

"Good." He shifted back, just slightly, so he could pull a small jewelry box from the pocket of his jeans. He opened it and revealed a two-carat diamond. "I love you. So you will marry me?"

She gaped at the ring, then brought her gaze to his hopeful face. When he smiled, she hugged him fiercely. "Yes!"

He slipped the ring onto her finger. "Now, weren't we on our way back to the bedroom?"

"For what? There's no bed back there."

He said, "Oh, you of no imagination. I have a hundred ways around that."

"A hundred, isn't that a bit ambitious?"

"Get used to it. I am a master, remember?"

"Yeah, you are," she said, and then she laughed. She was

getting married, going to make babies…going to make a *home—in Italy.*

With the man of her dreams.

Because finally, finally she was allowed to have dreams.

* * * * *

MILLS & BOON®
Hardback – July 2015

ROMANCE

The Ruthless Greek's Return	Sharon Kendrick
Bound by the Billionaire's Baby	Cathy Williams
Married for Amari's Heir	Maisey Yates
A Taste of Sin	Maggie Cox
Sicilian's Shock Proposal	Carol Marinelli
Vows Made in Secret	Louise Fuller
The Sheikh's Wedding Contract	Andie Brock
Tycoon's Delicious Debt	Susanna Carr
A Bride for the Italian Boss	Susan Meier
The Millionaire's True Worth	Rebecca Winters
The Earl's Convenient Wife	Marion Lennox
Vettori's Damsel in Distress	Liz Fielding
Unlocking Her Surgeon's Heart	Fiona Lowe
Her Playboy's Secret	Tina Beckett
The Doctor She Left Behind	Scarlet Wilson
Taming Her Navy Doc	Amy Ruttan
A Promise...to a Proposal?	Kate Hardy
Her Family for Keeps	Molly Evans
Seduced by the Spare Heir	Andrea Laurence
A Royal Amnesia Scandal	Jules Bennett

MILLS & BOON®
Large Print – July 2015

ROMANCE

HISTORICAL

MEDICAL

MILLS & BOON®
Hardback – August 2015

ROMANCE

The Greek Demands His Heir	Lynne Graham
The Sinner's Marriage Redemption	Annie West
His Sicilian Cinderella	Carol Marinelli
Captivated by the Greek	Julia James
The Perfect Cazorla Wife	Michelle Smart
Claimed for His Duty	Tara Pammi
The Marakaios Baby	Kate Hewitt
Billionaire's Ultimate Acquisition	Melanie Milburne
Return of the Italian Tycoon	Jennifer Faye
His Unforgettable Fiancée	Teresa Carpenter
Hired by the Brooding Billionaire	Kandy Shepherd
A Will, a Wish...a Proposal	Jessica Gilmore
Hot Doc from Her Past	Tina Beckett
Surgeons, Rivals...Lovers	Amalie Berlin
Best Friend to Perfect Bride	Jennifer Taylor
Resisting Her Rebel Doc	Joanna Neil
A Baby to Bind Them	Susanne Hampton
Doctor...to Duchess?	Annie O'Neil
Second Chance with the Billionaire	Janice Maynard
Having Her Boss's Baby	Maureen Child

MILLS & BOON®
Large Print – August 2015

ROMANCE

The Billionaire's Bridal Bargain	Lynne Graham
At the Brazilian's Command	Susan Stephens
Carrying the Greek's Heir	Sharon Kendrick
The Sheikh's Princess Bride	Annie West
His Diamond of Convenience	Maisey Yates
Olivero's Outrageous Proposal	Kate Walker
The Italian's Deal for I Do	Jennifer Hayward
The Millionaire and the Maid	Michelle Douglas
Expecting the Earl's Baby	Jessica Gilmore
Best Man for the Bridesmaid	Jennifer Faye
It Started at a Wedding...	Kate Hardy

HISTORICAL

A Ring from a Marquess	Christine Merrill
Bound by Duty	Diane Gaston
From Wallflower to Countess	Janice Preston
Stolen by the Highlander	Terri Brisbin
Enslaved by the Viking	Harper St. George

MEDICAL

A Date with Her Valentine Doc	Melanie Milburne
It Happened in Paris...	Robin Gianna
The Sheikh Doctor's Bride	Meredith Webber
Temptation in Paradise	Joanna Neil
A Baby to Heal Their Hearts	Kate Hardy
The Surgeon's Baby Secret	Amber McKenzie

MILLS & BOON®

Why shop at millsandboon.co.uk?

Each year, thousands of romance readers find their perfect read at millsandboon.co.uk. That's because we're passionate about bringing you the very best romantic fiction. Here are some of the advantages of shopping at www.millsandboon.co.uk:

* **Get new books first**—you'll be able to buy your favourite books one month before they hit the shops

* **Get exclusive discounts**—you'll also be able to buy our specially created monthly collections, with up to 50% off the RRP

* **Find your favourite authors**—latest news, interviews and new releases for all your favourite authors and series on our website, plus ideas for what to try next

* **Join in**—once you've bought your favourite books, don't forget to register with us to rate, review and join in the discussions

Visit **www.millsandboon.co.uk**
for all this and more today!